THE GENERAL'S WEAPONS

THE GENERAL'S WEAPONS

HEINOUS CRIMES UNIT™ BOOK FOUR

DANIEL SCOTT

Published by Marlowe & Vane
an imprint of LMBPN Publishing
PMB 196, 2540 South Maryland Pkwy
Las Vegas, NV 89109

Previously Published as *The General*
Version 1.01, January 2023
ebook ISBN: 979-8-88541-373-2
Print ISBN: 979-8-88878-006-0

THE GENERAL'S WEAPONS TEAM

Thanks to our JIT Readers

David Laughlin
Jan Hunnicutt
Daphne Reilly
Kelly O'Donnell
John Ashmore

Editor

Natale Wynne-Morril

For Heather Cowan. You and I both know the tremendous effort it took to edit this book. Thank you from the bottom of my heart.

The sun shone with such ferocity that it seemed to be taking revenge on the small Venezuelan town for some slight that no one could quite remember.

At one in the afternoon, the streets were nearly empty because the people couldn't handle the heat. Even the dogs knew it was smarter to seek shade than to venture out looking for scraps.

Christian Windsor sat in the back of an unmarked van with his sweat soaking through his shirt. The van's air conditioning couldn't keep up. He kept having to wipe his forehead and had already downed two bottles of water in the past hour.

There were four vans in total, two on the block opposite Christian's, and another sitting in front of him. He wondered if it was too many, but the local authorities had promised that the vans were nothing out of the ordinary. They all looked worn out. Christian's was almost broken.

He had stared out the front window as they drove, and

saw the Venezuelan police hadn't been exaggerating. Destroyed vans littered the city.

Christian didn't know for certain that Luke Titan was less than five hundred yards from him, but the probability was high. He had done something similar to this three other times in the past eighteen months, and each time he'd come up empty handed. In all three instances, Christian had been right that Luke Titan was there. However, he'd been wrong on his timing.

Not this time. Luke's here, and you're going to get him.

"How much longer?" he asked.

There were six people in the back of the van, and a driver and passenger were up front. The people in front wore painter's overalls. Those in the back wore heavy, bullet-proof armor and all had multiple guns holstered around their bodies. Each held an automatic weapon on their lap, and none of the men appeared to have a single ounce of fat on them.

"Ten minutes," the man to Christian's right said.

He didn't know these people. They were from other federal departments. Most likely the CIA, although Christian didn't concern himself with that. How these people had arrived here and where they came from was FBI Director Alan Waverly's job.

Christian's job was to capture Luke Titan.

The operation teams had ceased demanding that Christian remain in the States while their missions took place. Waverly had done a good job stating Christian's case and refusing their attempts to sideline him. He would be there when they either cuffed or killed Luke.

Christian used the towel on his lap to wipe the sweat from his brow. He wore the same tactical gear as those around him, although they hadn't equipped him with any automatic weapons. His pistol was strapped to his side. He'd practiced enough over the last year to pass as a decent shot.

The walkie-talkie sprang to life with a burst of static. "Bravo Team, come in, over."

"Bravo Team here, over," the man holding the walkie-talkie said.

"We have eyes on the target. He's crossing the street and heading to home base."

Christian stared at the bearded man next to him, desperately wanting to hear the words that would set the troops loose. The man didn't return his look.

"Copy. Distance? Over."

"Twenty feet, over."

The van pulled away from the curb. The person driving knew the plan of attack. Christian watched out the front window as they took a right.

Then he saw Luke.

Luke was wearing shorts and a light blue linen shirt. Flip-flops adorned his feet.

The van sped up and didn't pause for the curb, but jumped right onto it, causing everyone inside to bounce on the benches. Christian saw the other three vans flying across the street and jumping onto the apartment building's brown lawn.

"Subdue the target at all costs," the man to his right said into the walkie-talkie.

The van slammed to a stop and everyone piled out, every agent holding their automatic weapon in the ready position.

Christian stood as the last man jumped out, intent on following just as quickly, yet he paused. Luke had turned around and was watching the men dispersing from the vans. His hands weren't raised, and even from Christian's current distance, he could see the smile on his ex-partner's face.

Luke's gaze scanned his surroundings and somehow, despite the thirty men surrounding him, landed on Christian. He raised his hand and gave a small wave.

Christian jumped from the van and rounded its corner with his pistol raised and focused on Luke.

"Christian," his ex-partner called across the dead lawn. "If I didn't know better, I would think you miss me. You seem to be constantly trying to find me."

"*Kneel the fuck down!*"

Christian didn't know who screamed the order at Luke. He wouldn't take his eyes off the fugitive to figure it out, either. In a year and a half, they had never been this close to him. This was the first time Christian had laid eyes on Luke outside of video recordings since he had gutted him and stabbed him through the face.

"Christian, why are you doing this to yourself?" Luke asked. He hadn't knelt, nor made any other movement. "I told you I would come for you, didn't I? I said I'd see you soon. That I'd see all of you soon. Why are you inviting me before the time is right?"

"*Get the fuck down!*" someone else screamed.

Christian wouldn't have believed what happened next if

he wasn't there. Had someone told him what Luke had done, he would have thought it a myth to build up Luke's legacy. Christian *was* there, though, and neither his eyes nor mind lied to him.

Someone was moving in on Luke's right, perhaps the person who had just screamed at him.

Luke's gaze flashed to him, while the rest of his body remained facing Christian. The fully-armored agent stopped dead in his tracks. The entire group was closing in on Luke, encircling him, but that man stopped moving, caught in Luke's stare. He paused as the rest of the group continued tightening the noose.

Luke looked back at Christian.

"Okay, then," he said. "Have it your way."

Christian was twenty yards out from where Luke was standing, while the rest of the team was maybe five yards away.

Luke took a step back and raised his hands in the air.

"*Do not move!*" the first agent screamed. "*Don't take another fucking step!*"

"I'm not resisting," Luke said, moving back another step.

Christian's body was entranced by Luke's stare, but his mind wasn't. It saw what no one else did.

Luke was retreating, but there wasn't anywhere for him to go. There was *another* reason for it.

"*No!*" Christian shouted, just as Luke's foot reached the stoop of his apartment. "*Get back!*"

The agents heard Christian and paused briefly, a few of them looking over their shoulders. Luke stepped onto the stoop and other agents started screaming. Christian had set off panic in them. They yelled at Luke to get down, to surrender, to do everything except what the fuck he *was* doing.

"Christian!" Luke shouted above the fray. "You did this!"

Christian's mind categorized everything that happened next, even though his eyes couldn't keep up as it occurred. It was only later that he would be able to replay it back with a writer's attention to detail. Everything was perfectly in place as if he'd written the scene himself.

The yard exploded.

Christian watched as the dirt around the street sprayed outward, followed immediately by fire and crumbling concrete. The earth shook beneath him as if cannons had been installed beneath the street and then fired simultaneously. More flames erupted.

The men in front of Christian had no chance, and if he hadn't paused inside the van, he would have died as easily as they did. Their bodies were blown apart from the blasts, their limbs separating from their torsos like steamed chicken legs. Blood burst from ripped organs, coagulating with the dust in the air and creating a red, dirty mist.

Christian hit the ground and put his hands over his head, rolling onto his stomach as fire and shards of concrete rained down around him. He kept his eyes on Luke through the blood permeating the air and the destruction falling from the sky.

Shots were fired, ricocheting off the building behind him. Luke was somehow guarding Christian and saving him for a worse fate—nothing touched him.

The last explosion splattered dirt and body parts across

the ground. Christian tried to regain his feet, stumbling as he did and falling to a knee.

"Stop chasing me, Christian," Luke called. Christian could hardly hear his words through the ringing in his ears. "You'll have your chance soon enough."

CHAPTER ONE

Charles Twaller understood how people viewed his weight in the same way that a dog understands how people viewed it. It wasn't that he didn't care. He didn't even *think* about it. At 5'5" and 300 pounds, Charles made less than an impressive figure.

Charles didn't give a fuck about any of that. The last time he had worried about his weight was in the fifth grade when a punk kid had called him "fatso." The kid had gone home with a broken nose and an eye so swollen he couldn't see out of it for a week.

Twelve years later, Charles had gone back home after he'd graduated college and killed that punk kid. So, maybe, Charles had thought about it once more since fifth grade, but not fucking much.

Charles was twenty-one when he killed his first person. He was now thirty-five and didn't know how many people had died by his hand, let alone how many people had been murdered at his behest. The number was high.

Charles Twaller had a few mottos he lived by. He found

comfort in mottos. They were something that he could go back to when the world around him started getting stressful. He didn't walk around quoting them. He lived by them.

One of them was from a song he'd once heard. He didn't know what the song was or who'd sung it. He didn't give a fuck about that, either. It was the *words* that mattered.

And it's you I'll come for.

He'd thought about that lyric when he killed the punk kid, and every other time he'd committed murder. It helped focus his mind in those moments when life was about to be extinguished. Because Charles *wanted* to focus then, to soak it in.

He always giggled when he killed someone. Well, maybe not always, but quite often. It was the way they fell, awkwardly and without control. He couldn't help but giggle like a little girl when they collapsed, their fingers twitching and eyes staring at endless peace.

Charles wasn't a contract killer, and he didn't go around randomly offing people. He was very specific about the people he killed. Murder wasn't his business, but it was next door to his business.

He primarily dealt in guns but he sold weapons of all kinds. Tanks, pistols, automatic rifles. It didn't matter. He loved weapons. He had always loved them. The old saying was true. If you love what you do, you'll never work a day in your life. Charles loved every single day he woke up and got to transport guns.

He shipped them across state lines and international boundaries. He held them in warehouses and supplied them to warlords. Charles didn't care who needed them, or what their reasoning was. He cared that their money came through on time and securely.

Charles wasn't an idiot by any means. He had a degree in mathematics and had originally worked for an insurance company. The path upward would have been easy enough. He was smart, and his only family were his mother and sister. With no friends, he had all the time in the world to climb that corporate ladder. He just didn't see the return on investment being great enough. Even with the health-care and 401k match, how many years would it take him to reach a million dollars net worth?

Too-fucking-many.

Plus, he had liked killing that punk kid, and he certainly wouldn't have been able to do that in the actuary department of State Farm.

So, Charles had done what any entrepreneurial young man would do and started a side business. An illegal side business. Charles wasn't into imaginary lines the government said you couldn't cross. He wasn't into anyone's lines but his own.

He had another motto he liked.

Advance, whatever the costs.

So that's what Charles did.

He advanced.

Things moved quickly. At twenty-five, he was a fat man with a master's degree in math and a job at an insurance company. By thirty-five, he was a fat man with a master's degree and a five million dollar net worth, although the government only knew about five hundred thousand of it.

Still, Charles knew that sooner or later, the imaginary lines he cared nothing for would show up in bright red.

They would cease to be imaginary when he was facing three life sentences for trafficking weapons, not to mention the murders they would most likely pin on him. He could keep grinding and amassing great wealth, but in the end, bad deeds would be noticed.

There was his mother to think about, too. He sent money home every few months, and with no man in her life, his mom could use the cash.

Charles needed a score that would set him up for life. A score that would allow him to never need to worry about money again. Five million was a nice nest egg, but Charles wasn't sure that would keep him and Momma their entire lives. He could spend money like nobody's business, and if he was caught, the egg was fried.

One Friday at three in the afternoon, Charles was wondering if he'd finally found the score he needed.

The number of weapons currently stored in his warehouse was staggering, even for him. He didn't know if he'd ever seen this many guns in one place, and that was a powerful statement.

He'd walked around armories with African kings. But what he was looking at now…

Two bodyguards stood behind Charles, neither saying a word. Charles didn't want them to speak, and they knew it. The people who worked around the fat man quickly learned what he wanted, and if they didn't, they found themselves seeking new employment.

Charles knew their names because he knew everything about his business, but he would never say them aloud. He liked not calling anyone who worked for him by their name. It gave him a sense of importance. Guns, money, status. These were the things that mattered to him. Those, and mottos.

Mottos kept the world moving, after all.

The fifth shipment of weapons would arrive today and Charles was ready for them. He had his two bodyguards inside with him, but twenty more men were in the parking lot. The heat was awful outside and Charles liked making them wait in it.

Let 'em sweat.

The eighteen-wheeler rolled over the parking lot's gravel, and the sound of crunching rocks reached Charles' ears. He looked out the window. Sure enough, old Hector had arrived.

Charles waddled across the floor and out of the nearest door, exchanging the air conditioning for the intense heat. This Georgia sun was for the damned birds. Charles preferred his Boston home, but he went where the money compelled him.

This man wanted his weapons in south Georgia, so Charles, being the businessman he was, had arranged for it to happen.

The Mexican truck driver hopped out of the cab. Charles knew the man's name was David, but he liked to think of him as Hector. What kind of Mexican named their kid David?

Hector was about to die, although he didn't know it. It wasn't the best idea, and Charles understood that, but he didn't think he was dealing with the cartel. Hector was just some fuck that got hired for the job. He wasn't connected, so his death wouldn't cause any turmoil.

Plus, people knew it wasn't abnormal for drivers to die

around Charles Twaller.

"It's all there," Hector said as he crossed the gravel parking lot.

Charles extended his hand. "Good, good. How was the drive?"

"No problems."

The two shook hands and Charles turned to look at the back of the truck. His men were standing around it with dollies and forklifts ready to transfer the payload to the warehouse.

"Mind if I get the keys so the guys can get started?"

Hector pulled them from his pocket and handed them over.

"Here." Charles extended them to one of the body-guards without looking. The man took it from him and started walking toward the truck. "Shouldn't take us long. Want something to drink while they work?"

Charles stood about six inches shorter than the Mexican, so he had to look up as he spoke. The whole time his mouth was moving, his right hand was reaching into the back of his waistband and pulling the gun from it.

Hector's eyes widened as Charles pointed the black pistol at him. He didn't wait or beg, and Charles gave him some credit for that. The Mexican ran, turning tail and heading back to the truck's cab.

This will be good, Charles thought. He waddled forward, space opening between him and the soon-to-be-dead Mexican. It didn't matter. Charles didn't want to kill him on the gravel. The fall would be funnier if he reached the truck.

Hector leapt up the eighteen-wheeler's steps and swung

the door open. His foot slipped, and his shin collided with the metal step.

That's got to hurt, Charles thought.

He aimed the pistol and fired. The bullet clipped the side of the Mexican's head, blowing a chunk of his skull from it. The blood fell like a river no longer dammed, pouring out onto his neck, then his shoulder.

Hector froze, still holding onto the door. Charles couldn't see his eyes, but his pose made him look as if he was pondering something. Like maybe he'd forgotten his cellphone in the warehouse and needed to turn around.

Charles giggled.

The Mexican's hand slipped from the door handle and he slumped, continuing to slowly slide down. The blood kept running from his head, creating a red torrent down the side of his body.

He fell backward, his body hitting the ground with a *thump.* He stared straight up, his leg bent at the knee behind him, his other leg resting on the truck's cab.

That was funny. One leg bent and the other on the cab. That was *too* fucking funny.

Charles giggled again as his men went to work unloading the packages.

Charles hadn't spoken to the man who owned the cargo. Charles rarely spoke to anyone. Having underlings do it for him gave him insulation against actual conversations, which was important if the Feds came. Charles knew it wouldn't matter *that* much. He'd still spend the rest of his life behind bars, but perhaps his lawyers could bargain that down.

However, he needed to talk to the owner because with this many weapons, more money would be shelled out. Charles wanted, nay *needed*, a piece of it. Amassing capital quickly was the name of the game at this point. He was growing too big to escape notice much longer.

He sat down at a desk in the warehouse and watched as two men dragged the dead Mexican across the parking lot. His blood left a trail behind them, and for some reason, Charles giggled at that, too. He'd have the giggles for a while now. He did every time he killed someone.

"Focus, focus, focus, bucko," he said to himself.

He reached for the cellphone on the desk and scrolled through it. He had a direct number for his client, like always. He paid people to set up a direct number for each client that went through encrypted connections.

Charles didn't know how it worked, and he didn't need to. He only needed to know that it *did* work.

Charles hated the risk of speaking with any of his clients but knew he had to this time. Otherwise, he'd get instructions for the pickup, someone would show up, then the cargo would leave just as it had come. This was only a stopping point for the owner, at least as far as Charles knew.

He tapped his screen and the phone started ringing. He placed it on the desk, turning on the speakerphone.

"Hello?" his client answered.

"Hi," Charles said. "Do you know who this is?" The man should know. The number on the other end was very specific.

"I do."

Silence. Charles didn't like that one bit. The man said nothing else, letting his words hang in the air as if the conversation was already over.

"I wanted to speak to you about our exchange," Charles said, feeling uncomfortable for the first time that he could remember. He *never* felt uncomfortable, no matter the circumstances, and he'd dealt with nothing but criminals for a decade.

Yet those two words—*I do*—sounded so wrong.

"Okay," the man said, and nothing else.

Charles gave his spiel even as his mind reeled from the conversation's odd feeling. "I'd like to offer my services. I don't want to overstep boundaries, but with this much product I imagine you're going to need more help."

A pause came over the line and Charles wanted to fill it, but he clamped his teeth down until they hurt, refusing to let his instincts take over.

"That could be possible. Your name is Charles Twaller, right?"

His jaw dropped. The man shouldn't know his name. "How did you—"

"I like to know who I'm doing business with. I knew who you were before I hired you, so consider it a compliment. You're a very competent man, Mr. Twaller." The voice on the other side of the call was calm, eerily so.

Charles hated every word the man uttered. He wanted to hang up the phone. He couldn't, because this was real fucking money.

"What kind of services are you offering, Mr. Twaller?"

Anger flared inside the fat man at the use of his name—

so casually—as if he hadn't spent *years* insulating himself against just such a thing. He did his best to swallow the anger, just like he did the rest of his emotions.

"I can handle most anything you need, I think."

"You're not a man who thinks much. I thought you were a man who *knew* much."

Was this guy fucking with him? Was he trying to piss him off?

And it's you I'll come for, he thought, suddenly certain that he was going to kill this man at some point.

"I can handle what you need done," Charles said, his voice turning flat.

"You might be right. Perhaps we should discuss this in person? I won't go forward unless we do. What I'm asking is delicate."

"When are you available?"

"I can be at your warehouse in two days."

"Be here at eight in the morning."

Charles hung up without waiting for the man to say one more goddamn word.

He stared at the cellphone for a few seconds, his cheeks growing hot and his breathing coming more rapidly. His face twisted into a horrific grimace of red rage as he reached for the phone again. He slammed it onto the desk and the plastic edging broke, scattering to the floor. He brought the phone down again and again until there was nothing but wreckage in his hand.

One of the workers had stopped and was staring through the office window at his boss.

Charles glared at him and he went back to unloading.

CHAPTER TWO

"Three months, and we haven't heard anything." Alan Waverly stared across his desk at Christian and Tommy.

Christian nodded. There were things he could say, but none of them mattered. Tommy was quiet as well. He shifted a little in his wheelchair.

"There have been very few leads," Waverly continued.

Christian nodded again, deliberately not looking at Tommy. There had been a time not so long ago when this conversation would have been directed at his partner—at both of his partners—and Christian would have been the proverbial third wheel. No longer.

The meeting had been scheduled two weeks ago with the intention for Christian and Tommy to report on the single criminal they'd been chasing around the clock for months. They had their recommendations, were ready for Waverly's questions, and needed him to decide how the investigation would move forward. Christian and Tommy were at a crossroads and at odds on which way to proceed.

However, all of that was secondary for Christian. He

had something else he needed to bring up. Something more important in the long run.

"Sir," Christian said into the Director's silence, "it may be time to find someone else for my spot."

Alan Waverly leaned back in his chair and crossed his legs. He looked at Tommy. "Did you know he was going to say this?"

"Yes," Tommy whispered, which was the extent of his volume. The ability to speak louder was beyond him and would be for the rest of his life.

"You two are thick as thieves. Not a word from you on it, huh, Tommy? There was a time when I would have gotten a heads-up."

Christian thought Tommy would have shrugged, had he been able. He couldn't. He couldn't move at all. Two years ago, when Tommy could have moved, there was no way he would have shrugged at the Director for any reason, but time had changed all the men in this room.

Time, and Luke Titan.

"No one is replacing you, Christian, and I don't want to hear anything else about it."

"Sir, it's been three months."

"So?"

"I'm not sure I'm capable anymore."

Christian had thought long and hard about this conversation. He hadn't slept in forty-eight hours. His days had been spent chasing Luke and his nights were filled with contemplating what he was going to say in this meeting.

"Why aren't you capable?" Waverly asked.

"Every time I've been close to catching him, he's gotten

away. Three different South American countries where people died."

He didn't need to say anything else about *that*. Venezuela had been a disaster. Christian had gotten close two times before, and Luke had killed people during his escape both times. But not on the scale he had in Venezuela.

It had been an international blunder, with the cable news networks showing a cellphone recording of the explosions on a nearly endless loop.

"You carry those deaths on your shoulders, don't you?" Waverly turned to address Tommy before Christian could answer. "Do you agree with him? That he needs to give up his position?"

"No," Tommy said.

"And you've told him that?"

"Yes."

Waverly looked back to Christian. "You're not resigning, and I'm not replacing you. It's as simple as that."

Christian didn't know what to say. He felt nothing at the decision. He had stayed awake the past two nights, but he hadn't felt *anything* other than cold logic. Except that wasn't a feeling, more a frame of mind.

"Do you hear me?"

"Yes," Christian said.

"Good. You're staying. Three months doesn't mean anything, Christian. Do you know how long some of those guys have been on the most wanted list? *Years*. I have people still looking for them, too. I get a monthly read-out on Robert-fucking-Fischer, and he's been on the list since 2002. Three months is nothing."

Christian was silent but he held the Director's stare. He was able to hold anyone's gaze with ease since getting out of the hospital. Most of the time other people looked away first, although he thought that probably had more to do with the circular scar on his cheek.

"I'm not going to massage your ego, Christian, but no one else could have done what you've done. I'm not taking anything away from you, Tommy, but you've only been back six months. Christian, you've been at this for eighteen months, and you've nearly caught him three times. That's once every six damn months. If I could have you overseeing all of my most wanted criminals, I wouldn't *have* a most wanted list. Do you understand what I'm telling you?"

Christian nodded. It was odd hearing this from what amounted to the FBI's CEO, yet not feeling anything about it. He hadn't been at peace with leaving. He knew that he could never truly abandon the hunt for Luke. He may not be orchestrating the FBI's chase, but he would go after him forever if need be.

Two years ago, Luke had revealed his insane purpose. Christian had his own purpose now.

"Good. I don't want to hear anything else about it. You can resign when Luke is dead or captured. Now, let's talk about what leads we have."

"We have one report from a small Mexican town called Temisco," Tommy said. "It's about an hour or two outside of Mexico City. We sent down two agents at the beginning of the week."

"Any news from them?"

"Nothing substantial. They're just beginning to make their rounds. Trying to keep a low profile."

"Still no more letters?" Waverly asked.

"No," Tommy said.

Christian shook his head, recalling the last one Luke had sent verbatim, as he did all the others.

Dear Christian,

I wish I could say it was nice seeing you, but we both know I'd be lying. You're insatiable, Christian. Your need to find me— dare I say, kill me?—is impressive, if a bit frightening.

Do you still see the Other? The one who bleeds from his eyes and lives in your head? What does he say about your quest? Do you still think about Veronica? The love you lost, even while managing to keep her alive? I've tried to keep up with her, Christian, but the witness protection program has managed to shroud her even from me.

How about your mother? What does she think of you now? She once had a quirky and sensitive genius son. What does she have now? I imagine your quirkiness will never leave, but is your genius corrupted? Is your sensitivity dead?

I dream about you, Christian. Not often, but sometimes. It's always the same. The world is on fire around us both, buildings ablaze and people dying. Tommy is there, too. His life has already passed. You and I are looking at each other and we're not speaking. We only stare in silence, the heat baking us both.

What do you think that means?

The mind is a powerful tool, as you're well aware. Our mind tells us things through dreams. The original etymology of dream meant "sleeping vision." That's what I'm having when I sleep and you appear. A sleeping vision.

Fire is coming, Christian, and sooner than I wanted. It's going to rain down, and everything you know will burn. You brought this on yourself, with your inability to let me live on my own terms. Yes, I would have returned at some point and begun again, but perhaps I would have shown some mercy. We will never know now.

Mercy isn't coming with me. Only fire. Only blaze. Only chaos.

I will see you sooner than I had hoped, although I know not sooner than you hoped for.

Yours,

Luke Titan, MD, Ph.D., Special Agent for the Federal Bureau of Investigations, Top Ten of America's Most Wanted

Christian pushed the memory of the letter away. There had been other letters over the past two years, but Luke proclaiming his return and threatening Christian and everyone he loved had been the last one.

"Okay," Waverly said. "Give me a situation report. What are you guys thinking?"

"He's not lying," Christian said.

Waverly looked at Tommy. "You don't agree?"

"We have some disagreement between the two of us, sir," Tommy whispered.

"Let's hear it."

"Christian thinks Luke isn't coming alone. I think he is. I think he'll come and try to take us out one by one."

"Why do you think he'll bring a crew, Christian?"

There had been serious arguments about this between them. For the past three months, they had spent their time researching the possibilities, trying to decide how Luke would arrive. At the same time, both of them were hoping he wasn't already on the way. Or worse, already here.

All the research pointed to two possibilities, and Christian and Tommy were diametrically opposed on which one was correct.

"He said it in the letter. Everything is going to burn, and he can't do that by himself. Not the way he's describing it. If he comes alone, we won't end up standing in a ring of fire with buildings burning and people dying. It's too much for one man to achieve. Even him."

Waverly's brow furrowed as a quizzical look ran across his face. "You guys have been looking into this for months, and you're basing your conclusion on his letter?"

Christian nodded. He had nothing else to say. He spoke the truth, even if no one else saw it.

"What about your mansion?" Waverly asked. "Have you seen anything in there?"

Christian's mansion, which held everything he experienced in life and allowed him to make seemingly impossible leaps of logic, had changed dramatically. He wasn't afraid of it as he had been previously. He held no feelings about it one way or the other.

However, the top floor—the one dedicated to Luke—had been silent on this matter.

"No. There's nothing."

Waverly's eyes narrowed at Christian. After a moment, he turned to Tommy. "He telling you the same? That he's not seeing anything in his head?"

"Yes," Tommy whispered.

"I'm right here," Christian said. "You're accusing me of lying with me sitting right across from you."

Waverly smiled and leaned back in his chair. "It wouldn't be the first time you've been deceptive, would it?"

Christian said nothing.

"How would he get a crew of people?" Waverly continued.

"There are a couple of ways. He could hire them, although that doesn't feel right to me. The other way would be to create a cult of people dedicated to him who would do whatever he wants."

"That sure as hell sounds like him," Waverly said.

"I don't buy it," Tommy said. "If Luke were amassing a group around him, it would be hard to hide it for long. The entire world knows his face. He isn't like the others on the most wanted list. He's Luke Titan. He can't set up a compound without attracting the authorities, even in a foreign nation."

"That's true," Waverly said.

These arguments were old between Tommy and Christian. They'd hashed everything out over countless nights and still ended up on opposite sides.

"He's not coming by himself," Christian said. "He did that last time, and now he's on the run. When he returns, he's bringing people with him."

Waverly was silent for a second, thinking. Christian admired the man's decisiveness and knew that he was coming to a decision on which path to take. There were no other options that either Christian or Tommy could map out.

"I'm with Tommy, Christian. What you're suggesting is too difficult, and I don't think he's had enough time to build up a cult. Two years might be long enough if he wasn't running from country to country." Waverly turned to Tommy. "Let's hear your plan."

CHAPTER THREE

The waitstaff didn't like the gringo who came in once a week. They didn't dislike him either. He was quiet, always paid his bill, and always tipped well. In a small Mexican town like the one the restaurant was in, that should have been all anyone needed to do to be treated like a king.

The gringo was different. He wore a small sombrero and sunglasses when he came to the restaurant, and he always sat in the same spot on the porch, at a table nearest the street. He always faced the street and usually brought a pad of paper and a pen with him. Sometimes he wrote. Sometimes he watched the people passing by on the street.

He would eat from the basket of chips placed in front of him and drink red wine. Three glasses before he asked for his tab and then left.

El Fantasmo Blanco.

The White Ghost.

A cook had given him that name, an older bald man who had watched the gringo enter and exit the restaurant numerous times. The cook kept his distance and advised everyone else to do the same.

"*No está bien. En aquí,*" he said, tapping his temple. *He's not right. In here.*

The waitstaff saw it as well, even if they hadn't been able to voice their feelings. It was in the way El Fantasmo Blanco carried himself. It was in the way he looked at the waitstaff when he occasionally removed his sunglasses. He focused when he asked for something in perfect Spanish, but he looked *through* them.

The waiters and waitresses treated him with respect, but they kept their distance. They appreciated the tips, but they would have appreciated it just as much if he'd stopped coming in.

The ghost had been busy the past few days, even if no one at the restaurant knew it.

He was preparing to leave, and as he sat down today, he had prepared for something else as well. He pulled his pen and paper out, setting them down in the shadow of the umbrella above. The sun was blazing, but the umbrella would keep its ruthless nature from annoying the gringo.

The chips came first, and then the wine. The waiter did not ask what the ghost needed. It wasn't necessary.

The ghost looked out at the street, watching people move to and fro. Then he turned and motioned for the waiter to come back.

The ghost spoke in Spanish. "There is a cook inside. Will you bring him to me?"

The waiter's eyebrows rose slightly, but he kept his countenance. "Si, señor."

The ghost went back to staring at the street as the waiter did his bidding.

A few minutes passed before the cook walked out onto the patio. He was wiping his hands with a rag, and his face was still as he approached the table.

"*Hablas Inglés?*" the ghost asked.

"Yes. Some."

"Good. Have a seat."

The cook pulled the chair out closest to the street and sat.

"What is your name?" the ghost asked.

"Torez."

"Good. You didn't lie."

The ghost studied the cook. There was fear inside him, but he hid it well. He had seen a lot in his life, hardships unimaginable to many people north of the border. He might be sitting in front of a ghost, but it might not have been his first time.

"Last week," the ghost continued, "you stepped out here to smoke. You saw me and left, heading to the front. Why?"

The cook swallowed. "I do not like you."

The white man smiled. "Now that I can understand. Why don't you like me?"

"You are evil."

The ghost took off his glasses. He leaned back in his chair and crossed one leg over the other. "How do you know?"

"Your eyes. They tell your soul to the world. Or, they would if you had one. You do not."

The ghost nodded, his face still as he turned to observe the street. He was silent for a moment, then said, "I've been following you over the past few days. It bothered me that you ran off so quickly last week, and I needed to understand what you knew." He turned back to the cook. "I don't think you know anything, so I'm going to tell you—"

"No, *señor*. No," the cook interrupted.

"Hush, Torez,' the ghost whispered. He leaned forward and placed his elbows on the table. "My name is Luke Titan. I'm unsure if you know the name, but the information could be very valuable for a man such as yourself. I'm leaving this place soon, so your window of opportunity is closing rapidly. If you wish to sell that name, you will need to do it quickly. However, if you do sell it, you will die soon after. Much too soon to enjoy any of the money you would have earned."

The cook worked the rag between his hands.

The ghost pulled an envelope from his front shirt pocket. It was relatively heavy. Its contents couldn't be seen.

"In here is $100,000. I buy your silence with that money. If you take it, no one will ever hear my name from you."

"And if I don't take it?" the cook asked.

"Then your silence hasn't been bought."

The two stared at each other for a second, the envelope in between them.

"You're soulless. I cannot accept money from you. I will not speak your name."

The ghost looked for a second longer, then placed the envelope back in his pocket. "Your choice."

The cook's jaw tightened for a second at the loss of

such a great sum of money, but his face quickly resumed its normal state.

"Okay, then. We understand each other," Luke Titan said.

The cook nodded and stood. He walked back into the restaurant, leaving the ghost alone.

Luke looked back at the street. He wasn't surprised the old man hadn't taken his money. The cook's fear was genuine, and superstition didn't die as one grew older. For him to have accepted such a large amount of money would have been akin to selling his soul.

Luke liked that the man had held firm. His soul wasn't for sale. Neither was Luke's.

He was heading back to Georgia tomorrow, back to the world he'd left behind. Christian had been relentless, and that was something else Luke liked. Christian wanted to catch Luke above all else.

Luke hadn't been ready to return, but Christian was yet again forcing his hand much as he had back in Mackenrow's house. He hadn't wanted things to unfold the way they had. There were *plans* that should have taken place and hadn't because Christian had been too fast, at least mentally.

Now he was proving too fast yet again. Forcing Luke to act before he was ready.

No matter. He would go back to the States. Back to Georgia. Back to Tommy and Christian. He would bring them what they so desperately wanted.

CHAPTER FOUR

Charles watched the man step from his car from his vantage point inside the warehouse. He had fifty men here today, all of them armed with automatics. It was overkill and he knew it, but he didn't care.

His client had left him feeling uncomfortable, and he hadn't been able to find out a damned thing about him.

The man was a ghost, if he existed at all. Perhaps the man he was looking at was simply lost and had pulled into the old warehouse, planning on stretching his legs before heading out. That made as much sense as the calm man on the phone showing up.

Charles had used all his considerable power to try and figure out who he was dealing with, but he had learned nothing until this very moment, as the man stood beneath the hot summer sun.

He wore an Atlanta Braves baseball cap, sunglasses, and a closely cropped beard. He was dressed in blue jeans and a button-down shirt, which was tucked in.

The man was thin, but Charles' eyes were sharp, and he

could see the muscle beneath the shirt. Charles didn't give one fuck about muscles, not when he had fifty M-16s pointing at the man, but it was still good to know.

Charles took the elevator down and walked out onto the gravel parking lot. The guards followed him, all fifty of them. They knew exactly what Charles wanted. The man in the baseball cap needed to understand who was in charge, and where the power resided in this relationship.

The guards fanned out around him as he headed toward the black car. The sunglasses hid the man's eyes from Charles, but he appeared unbothered by the armed men walking toward him.

"How was your trip?" Charles asked when he reached the car.

"It was fine. You brought quite a crowd." He was looking up at the sky. "I've missed Georgia."

The black sunglasses reflected Charles' face at him. Their opaque lenses blocked the man's thoughts but seemed to be speaking their own.

Nothing you do can hurt the person behind these.

"I've got enough men to solve any problem you have."

"Shall we go inside?" the man asked as he scanned the guards.

"Sure, I'll show you your product."

Charles led the way inside, listening carefully as the man walked behind him. He hadn't broached the subject of the man's name yet, but he would soon.

"Here you are," Charles said as they entered the lower floor of the warehouse.

Large boxes atop wooden pallets covered half of the ten thousand-foot square warehouse, creating massive squares.

An arsenal.

"It looks like a lot now that I'm standing in front of it," the man said, his voice as calm now as it had been outside. He was goddamn staring at an armory larger than most small countries possessed, and he sounded like he was ordering coffee.

"Before we go any further," Charles said as he turned, "I need to know who I'm dealing with."

"You weren't able to find out?"

"Not everything," Charles said, lying and hating that he had to. *And it's you I'll come for,* he thought.

"That's good." The man hadn't turned to look at Charles. He stood gazing at the boxes.

Charles saw two options in front of him. He could kill this person right now and deal with the consequences, or he could play this fucking game and see where it led.

He felt the gun pressing against his back, burning like a brand. It *wanted* to be freed and allowed to put a bullet through the man's goddamn baseball cap.

Charles smiled at the thought of a sudden hole opening up in the side of his head. He giggled, envisioning the blood bubbling down the man's shoulder.

"Something funny?" the calm man asked without turning.

"No, not yet," Charles said. "Now, who are you?"

"This is a delicate subject for me, Mr. Twaller. I'm not trying to be coy, but I need to stress why it's so delicate. You see, if my identity were revealed to certain entities, my life would be over." The man turned, removing his sunglasses as he faced Charles.

Everyone was taller than Charles, and this man was no

exception. He looked down at Charles with brown eyes that were harder than baked brick.

"I want to make sure that you won't be tempted to tell such entities, Mr. Twaller. A man in your position could probably arrange to be paid without revealing his identity."

Charles swallowed, his lips pursing. "I don't care if you're Jimmy fucking Hoffa. I didn't get to where I am by ratting."

"It's nothing personal."

The man smiled, his white teeth looking closer to those of a great white shark's than a human's. A chill ran down Charles' back and his nipples grew hard.

"My name is Titan, Mr. Twaller. Dr. Luke Titan. Have you heard of me?"

Charles saw through the beard and the hat for the first time. Perhaps he'd had some cosmetic work done on his face, but Charles wasn't sure how he'd failed to recognize him.

Titan had been all over the news a few years ago. His face had been as famous as the President's for a little while. Charles laughed when he realized he'd almost killed one of the most wanted men in the country. He'd almost put a fucking bullet right through his skull, and *that* was hilarious.

Charles giggled, his big belly bouncing above his belt. "Oh, God," he said in between his laughter. "You really are Luke Titan."

The man kept smiling. "I really am."

Charles was trying to talk through his laughter. He was out of breath, yet he couldn't stop giggling. "I bet you want to go to war, don't you? That's what all this is for! You want the blood to wash right up to the goddamn FBI's doorstep!"

Luke's thoughts wandered as he drove. He had picked the right man for the job, even if he hadn't been certain based on the man's resume. Charles Twaller's curriculum vitae read like Luke imagined an arms dealer's might if there was a Harvard and Goldman Sach's for arms dealers.

Mr. Twaller worked with all the right people and had an impeccable reputation, if he disregarded that he was perhaps a bit too freewheeling with the drivers who delivered his cargo.

The murders of the drivers were what had sold Luke on Charles Twaller. Luke didn't want a Harvard type in charge of what came next. He needed someone with a bit more...unpredictability.

The dead drivers made Luke think Mr. Twaller would be that man. He was buttoned down and professional all the time, except for the times when he would kill in cold blood. He had killed other people and even been to war with a rival once. But all of that was business. The dead drivers weren't business. They were pleasure.

Luke had chosen him to hold his weapons in the hope that he might take the next contract.

Mr. Twaller was perfect, and Luke saw it as the short, fat man giggled like a schoolgirl, surrounded by millions of dollars in guns.

The past two days had been long. Luke had traveled from Mexico to Los Angeles, and finally to Atlanta. He'd rented a vehicle and traveled to southern Georgia, and now he was driving back to the city.

Luke felt no exhaustion. He was excited because he was going to lay eyes on Christian tonight.

He'd seen his old partner a few times over the past two years, but each had been fleeting and unfulfilling. Tonight, he would have longer to look at Christian. To see the scar he'd left on his face.

Luke had never felt at home. He's never felt displaced, either. However, perhaps for the first time in his life, he felt a sense of *returning*.

Not quite to home, but close.

As Luke headed to Christian, Charles looked on as his workers unpacked the boxes. Five teams of five were using crowbars to reveal the weapons shining black like oil underneath the lights above.

Charles' mind was looking far into the future. What was being asked of him would not be easy, and there was a large chance that he would be caught or killed. He had to be diligent in his preparations if he was to make it out of this relatively unscathed.

A lot of people were going to die. The certainty of death didn't bother Charles at all, only the difficulty it would cause when it came to recruitment. The higher the risk, the higher the price per head.

Titan wanted numbers by the end of the week, but Charles already knew them. For most people, the final tally would have been prohibitively high, but Charles believed Titan could find the cash.

Funding would be there. Charles needed to provide the soldiers for his war, but he could do it. He had a pipeline of mercenaries.

All-out war on the Federal Bureau of Investigation was what Luke Titan wanted.

The strategy was the key to this contract. It would need to be quick and ferocious. Attacks that took place over a few days, inflicting the maximum amount of carnage, and then Charles' army would disappear.

What was left of it, anyway.

CHAPTER FIVE

Christian pulled Luke's Tesla into the driveway. He'd been driving the vehicle for a year and a half, but he still didn't think of it as his.

Waverly had made sure Christian got the car. For years, Christian had taken ride-sharing vehicles rather than driving himself. When he'd left the hospital this last time, he'd asked Waverly for the vehicle.

"After what he did to me, I want Luke's car," he'd told Waverly. "Is it impounded?"

Waverly's brow had furrowed. "I'm not sure."

"Can you get it for me? Assign it to my department?"

Waverly had stared without speaking for a few seconds, judging the reasoning behind Christian's request.

The car had arrived at the Atlanta FBI office three days later.

Christian stepped from the vehicle and went to his mailbox. There were a few pieces of mail but no decapitated heads, which was always a blessing.

Lord, if he stopped and thought about all the things he'd seen, he might never be able to start moving again.

He didn't agree with Tommy's plan, and he didn't agree with Waverly's decision, either. He might be the leader of his unit, but in the end, he had to follow orders. At one point, Christian might have shirked those duties, those orders, but no longer.

He and Waverly had come to an understanding in the hospital while Christian debriefed him on everything that had taken place with Luke inside Mackenrow's house. The FBI Director hadn't wavered in the slightest as Christian spoke with the knife hole carved deep in his face. He'd looked Christian dead in the eye for hours, then retired to the lobby when Christian needed rest.

The plan of attack had been developed over the next few weeks. Christian had nothing to do with it. He was too busy recovering from Luke's brutal attack. Waverly had come back, sitting down in the same chair and looking at Christian with eyes that said they would die before they quit.

"You're being reassigned," he'd told Christian. "You're no longer in the Exceptional Crimes Unit. You're being reassigned to the Targeted Individuals Program. You are the sole agent on the team as of right now. Your unit's mandate is to find Luke Titan. *He* is the targeted individual. This unit is a line item all to itself on my budget, and the President himself signed off on it. Do you have any qualms?"

Christian had shook his head, pain flaring in his cheek as it did every time he moved.

"Good. The doctors say you'll be ready to return to work in five months. I expect you there."

"What about until then? Who's going to be looking for him?"

Waverly smiled. "I thought you might ask that. Here." He pulled a laptop from his bag. "Don't get caught with it," he said as he placed it on the bed next to Christian.

And thus, the Targeted Individuals Program had been born. Tommy had joined eleven months later. His recovery had taken much longer, and with much less success.

They had one other agent in the unit. Waverly had assigned Simone Goodfriend to the unit without acknowledging any debate in the matter from Christian and Tommy. That had been the right move, if the annoying one.

Christian arrived home and went straight to his bed. He opened his laptop and rested it on his stomach. He'd had the same routine since college when he was working on multiple degrees instead of chasing criminals.

He pulled up the email outlining the plan of action that Waverly had sent after the meeting.

They were so wrong on this, but he didn't know how to make anyone see it. Luke wasn't coming by himself, but without more proof, Waverly was taking that route. In truth, Tommy's idea *was* more logical. No one believed it was possible to amass the resources in the time it would take to arrange something as massive as Christian suspected.

Christian stared at the computer for a few minutes, then shut it down. He rose from his bed and headed for the kitchen, pulling his phone out as he went.

He hadn't called his mother for a few days. She hadn't called him either. He noticed it as surely as she noticed *his* absence. Each of them were remaining silent for different reasons.

Christian had always found it hard to relate to people, but never his mother. Not until Luke shoved a knife through his face, at least. Now, speaking to her hurt them both.

Everything changed, he thought as he pulled up her number on the phone. *Everything changed, and there's only one thing you can do about it. Find Luke and kill him.*

But would that change anything? No.

He held the phone and stared at his mother's number for a moment, not quite ready to dial.

Everything from the scar on his cheek to his inability to communicate with his mother could be traced back to Luke. The person he had trusted, looked up to, admired.

Christian had missed the truth. Stared at it for years and saw nothing but what Luke wanted him to see. Look what happened because of it. A lot of people had died, and Christian knew that a lot more were about to.

He pressed the call button, forcing that thought from his head.

"Hey, honey," his mother answered.

"Hey. Sorry I haven't called. It's been a busy few days at work. Waverly came into town."

"No problem. I know you call when you can."

Silence fell over the line. Christian hated how great the distance had grown between the two of them. He'd always felt that distance with others, but never with her. She was his lifeline to the world, what had kept him connected for so long.

"How are you?" he asked finally.

"I'm good. Trying not to worry about you. It's easier said than done."

"Why are you worrying?"

"You really need to ask that?" she said.

"Yes. I'm fine. I'm in no danger."

"There's more danger than the physical kind, Christian. But you know that."

Silence again. All of Christian's brainpower, and yet his mother could shut him down with two sentences.

He stepped outside onto his porch and closed the door behind him. "Luke is coming back."

"How do you know?"

Christian chuckled without mirth. "He wrote a letter telling me. He isn't too big on secrecy, at least on some things."

"So, you might not be safe physically, either."

"I…" He wouldn't lie to her, so he let the sentence die. There was no safety from Luke, and Christian knew that. There was only relentless attack, and the hope that he could be more brutal than his nemesis.

"Christian, I've got to get some food out of the oven. Will you promise me you'll be careful?"

He heard the tears in her voice. She rarely showed such emotion. She had always been strong for him and helped him to navigate the world.

Why does she cry, Christian? Because that person no longer exists. The person on the phone isn't her son, but Luke's.

"I will, Mom," he said.

The moon perched high in the sky, casting its light upon demon and saint alike without judgment of worth.

Luke had once been called a demon. Lucy Speckle had given him that title before slitting her own throat. Luke had no use for terms like demon or saint. If pressed, he would align himself closer to the saintly class.

He stepped inside Christian's front door and closed it behind him. He breathed in deeply, smelling Christian's scent. He hadn't realized how much he had missed it until now.

The house was silent. Luke could make out Christian's breathing pattern. His old partner was asleep, luckily. He would have still come even if that wasn't the case.

His footsteps made no sound on the hardwood flooring. Very few people were aware of the stealth with which Luke could move, but he was a predator through and through.

He moved through the house without stopping, his eyes roaming as he walked. The silent alarm was most certainly going off, alerting the police to the intrusion. That gave Luke about seven minutes before blue lights and sirens filled the quiet neighborhood.

Luke had seen the alarm when he stepped in, and smiled at it. Christian knew Luke would show up one day. He'd installed a tailor made alarm so that it *wouldn't* ring in the house just in case Luke might miss it.

He didn't miss anything. That was what made him so deadly.

Luke reached Christian's bedroom. The door was

standing open. He stepped inside and walked to the edge of the bed.

Christian was on his back. Moonlight filtered through the blinds, creating just enough illumination for Luke to see Christian's face when he leaned in to stare at the boy. Was he still a boy? Or had what he had done to him pushed him over the threshold into manhood?

Christian's angry scar would be red in light, but it was dark and forbidding now. Luke had put that scar there. The knife had left other unseen damage as well, damage that stretched much deeper than any blade could reach.

Luke stared with the intensity of a wolf, although he wasn't aware of the cruelty his face wore. For once, he was lost in his head, moved by the sight of the man he'd done so much for.

Minutes passed before Luke's mind overpowered his emotions, ripping him from his thoughts and alerting him to the time.

Luke moved his thumb to hover over Christian's scar without touching the man's skin. He stood there with his thumb blocking his view of the red circle, giving Christian the appearance of smooth skin once again.

He dropped his hand back to his side and left the house as silently as he'd arrived.

The sirens screeched through Christian's dream, breaking it apart as a sledgehammer would glass.

His eyes opened and he swung his feet out of bed

almost immediately. He pulled out his service weapon when he heard someone call from the front door.

"Dr. Windsor, I'm Officer Bradley Romaine with the Atlanta Police Department. Are you inside?"

Christian's mind raced to understand what was happening. He was missing too many variables to say anything with certainty.

He called out to the officer, "I'm in my bedroom. I'm uninjured. Can you tell me what happened?"

He heard footsteps falling across the floor and placed his weapon on top of the nightstand.

The police officer turned the corner, his gun raised. "Dr. Windsor? I need to see some identification."

"Sure, but I need to get it for you. Is that okay?" Christian crossed the room when the officer nodded and grabbed his wallet off the top of his chest-of-drawers. "Can I toss it to you?"

The officer nodded again and Christian flipped his ID toward him. The officer caught it easily, holstering his weapon after looking at the name and photo on the plastic card.

"Thanks," he said, crossing the room. "Your alarm went off, and my partner and I were dispatched here. He's securing the perimeter."

Christian's mind was still muddled from the abrupt awakening. "I was sleeping. You're saying it went off?"

"Yes, sir. It alerted us approximately ten minutes ago. You didn't hear anything? No one's been here? Did you have an overnight guest who left and set it off?"

Christian looked at the floor, his eyes narrowing. He

ignored the questions. His eyes flicked back up after a second. "The door was open? The front door?"

"Yes, sir."

"Romaine? Interior secure?" the partner called from the front door.

"Everything's secure," Romaine called over his shoulder.

The other officer walked across the house, joining the two in Christian's bedroom.

"Sir," Romaine continued. "Were there any overnight guests?"

"No, no," Christian said. He walked past the two of them without saying anything else. He hustled down the hallway toward the front door. He heard the two officers following behind.

Christian rounded the corner to the foyer, where the door still stood ajar.

It had been open when the police arrived. His alarm had gone off, bringing the police to his house. Yet no one was here. Just him.

Christian stood with his back to the two officers as they entered the foyer.

"Sir?"

Christian closed his eyes and sighed.

"Go ahead and file your report. The FBI will take over once you're finished."

———

Last night was the first time Christian had slept in four days—or it was supposed to be. He hadn't, of course, fallen back asleep once the police arrived.

He showed up to the office at seven in the morning. He hadn't shaved, his hair was a mess, and his shirt and tie were a poor mimic of someone wanting to look professional. Christian didn't care about any of it.

He took the elevator down to subbasement C. He and Tommy no longer worked above ground. Waverly had given Christian the subbasement in the new unit's beginning when Christian had told him he wanted to work alone. The Director had not objected.

There were three offices set up in the subbasement, one for each of the people in the unit.

Christian saw Tommy's office light was on. He crossed the small interior floor to Tommy's door.

"Luke is back."

Tommy's eyes were the only part of him that could move easily. They flashed to Christian as his fingers did a slow dance on his wheelchair controls, turning the chair to face Christian.

"What?" he whispered.

It was lucky he could talk at all. Luke had stabbed Tommy "perfectly" in his neck, severing his spinal cord without killing him. Tommy's vocal chords, through a lot of diligence and hard work on his part, had come back to him, although his voice would always be weak. They'd never return to their former state. Nothing about Tommy would.

"Luke came to my house last night. The alarm went off, but he left before the police showed up."

Tommy backed his wheelchair up from the computer monitor. "Slow down. How do you know it was him?"

Christian stepped inside the office, uttering a high

laugh that was born of stress and exhaustion. "Who else could it be, Tommy? Veronica didn't suddenly show up to see me and leave before I woke up. Nothing was taken. Nothing was disturbed. The lock wasn't even damaged. The cops said it didn't appear to have been messed with at all."

"Then how did he get in?"

"He picked it without leaving any trace." Christian paced back and forth in front of Tommy's desk. "He's here, and he wanted me to know there's nothing I can do about it."

"Waverly will want to hear about this."

"I'll send him the police report. I got them to give me a copy before they filed."

"You think it lends support to my theory? That he's coming alone?"

Christian stopped walking and faced the whiteboard at the front of the office. "If it did, wouldn't he have killed me?"

"No. It wouldn't have been dramatic enough. It wouldn't have caused enough *chaos*. No one would know Luke did it. They might suspect, but there'd be no proof."

"Are you worried he might come after you next?"

Christian didn't turn around at the soft laughter he heard.

"Seeing Luke again would be a damned relief, buddy. I don't think he'd let me live this time, and that's not necessarily such a bad thing."

"You've got to go home."

Tommy listened to Simone Goodfriend chastising Christian, smiling inside even if he couldn't on the outside. The two of them stood in Tommy's office, staring at each other as if he wasn't there.

"I'm not going to watch you pacing around here all day because you didn't get any sleep. I knew this shit was coming. I've seen it the past week. You've got to go home and sleep."

"I'm fine," Christian said.

"You're not fine. Look at you. You look homeless. When was the last time you slept?"

"It's not important."

"It certainly is important," Simone said. "When you don't sleep, you start acting weird. It's too close to the weekend for me to have to deal with your oddness. Go home and sleep."

Tommy knew what she meant, even if her words didn't say it, per se. She didn't like Christian's countenance when he was lacking sleep, but that wasn't her real concern. She knew Christian needed sleep for his own sake, and *that* was what she cared about. The woman was brash, but Christian knew as well as Tommy that she meant well.

"I'm not going home," he said. "I don't know if you've forgotten, but Luke was in my house last night. I don't think that's the safest place for me."

"Fine. Go to my house. Sleep there."

Christian opened his mouth to say something. He paused, a small smirk growing on his face.

Simone didn't smile. "Go on. Here are my keys."

Christian shook his head and walked past her without taking them from her hand.

"He's ridiculous," Simone said once Christian was out of the room.

She didn't wait for an answer before she followed him, intent on badgering him until he acquiesced.

Tommy let out a sigh after the room emptied. He'd gotten to the office around five that morning, wanting to look at their plan with a fresh set of eyes. He'd been able to get about two hours of work in before Christian showed up.

It was eight now, and Christian would certainly email Waverly before he left the office. If he *did* leave. These power struggles weren't *always* decided in Simone's favor.

Tommy needed silence to process everything Christian had told him. He preferred silence more and more nowadays. The only two people he spent time around were Christian and Simone, but sometimes he didn't even want to be around them.

Now was one of those times.

Tommy used his right index finger to propel his wheelchair across the room. He hooked the front right portion of the chair into the sliding glass door's crevice, then moved the wheelchair forward. The door glided closed.

He turned the chair around, but he didn't go back to his desk. He wanted to think about Luke.

His relationship with Luke was odd, to say the least. He spent the vast majority of each day hunting the man, thinking about nothing other than him. Yet he never actually thought *about* Luke. He thought about catching him, about trapping him, about any number of things relating to his capture. Rarely did he think on the actual man.

That part of Tommy's life was over. In some ways, it felt like it had happened to someone else entirely. He had decided early in his recovery that he wouldn't venture down that road. To go there was to die, if not physically, then certainly spiritually.

Alice wasn't coming back. He couldn't reverse time and take back the bullet Luke had put in her skull. There was no way to give him his voice back, or the ability to move.

He couldn't get any of it back, and thinking about Luke reminded him of that. Tommy didn't want to be reminded of the man he once was, nor the person he'd turned into. So, he focused on work, and left thinking about Luke to Christian.

He couldn't do that right now. Waverly would have questions about what Christian thought had happened last night, and Tommy would need to be prepared.

More than that, if Luke was back, then it didn't matter what Tommy had told Christian about it being a relief.

He would come for Tommy. He'd come for them all. Tommy wasn't afraid of death. Perhaps what he'd told Christian was true. Perhaps he did wish for death. However, he didn't want to meet it before seeing Luke meet his own. That was what motivated Tommy. The hope of seeing Luke lying with his eyes open and blood leaking from his mouth. He hadn't told anyone that, but he didn't think he needed to either.

Tommy Phillips didn't have a lot to live for anymore, and that should have been plain to everyone.

CHAPTER SIX

"We're ready," Charles said into the phone.

"Okay. I trust you have everything you need? The money will clear in the next hour. Feel free to wait until after it does before beginning."

Thanks for your permission, you fuck, Charles thought.

"Once the money clears, I'll have everything I need."

"Where do you plan on watching from?" Titan asked.

"I have an area in my house dedicated to making sure everything goes as planned."

"Would you mind if I watched with you?"

Charles didn't want to watch *anything* with this man. He didn't want to be anywhere near him, not unless he could hold a gun to his forehead. What was he going to say? The man was paying with cash. If he wanted to sit on Charles' lap while the crew gunned down FBI agents, then that's what he'd get.

The money was just too good.

"No, that's fine. My assistant will make sure you get the address. You'll need to be here by five in the morning."

"Certainly," Titan said.

"Okay. I'll see you then."

Charles hung up and stood up from his kitchen table.

He resisted the urge to pace and remained standing where he was with his hands formed into fists like an extremely fat twelve-year-old. Red anger crept up his face, having already laid claim to his neck.

"*Motherfucker!*" he shouted, spittle flying from his mouth and landing on the table.

He didn't like being played like a fiddle, and that's exactly what Titan was doing. Titan, with all his genius, had to *know* Charles wanted nothing to do with him. Yet he would be at Charles' home tomorrow morning.

Don't kill him. Don't do it. Not until this is finished and your money is right. There's you and Mom to think about. Your goddamn sister, too.

The red slowly faded from his cheeks, leaving them pale and flabby. He waddled across his kitchen, through the dining room, and into his living room. The large coffee table that sat in front of the two couches was cleared of any decorations at the moment. A map of the United States with four tiny, red circles drawn on it lay across the surface.

These were the four spots they would attack tomorrow. The mercenaries would be in position. Arrival routes had been planned, as well as paths out. The routes out would be much more difficult to navigate. Perhaps even impossible.

Charles didn't know. He didn't care, either. The mercenaries had already been paid. If they died, then arrangements would be made to send their payment to whomever they'd designated. He didn't give a goddamn if their kids or wives or Chinese sex slaves got it.

If it had been possible, he would have pocketed the cash of every man who died. It wasn't, of course. They knew they most likely would die, so these desperados wouldn't have joined without the ability to leave a check for someone else.

The problem Charles had wasn't with routes or enough men.

The problem was he had no end goal. Titan hadn't given him one, and when he asked about it, the mother-fucker had only said, "Let's see how many we can kill. That's a good goal, no?"

Sure, a great goal. Hell, Charles liked watching people die, but that wasn't a goddamn reason to go to war with the government.

Charles had always known he was a bit off. Different than other people. You didn't exactly get a hard-on from murder and think you were *normal*.

This man, Titan… He was truly insane.

Veronica Lopez always knew Luke would come for her again. Even as she signed the papers erasing her old life, she'd said, "None of this matters. When he wants me, he'll get me."

Veronica Lopez was part of the witness protection program, although she had yet to testify against anyone.

FBI Director Alan Waverly had explained it to her in cold, calm detail. They didn't have the resources to follow her for the rest of her life, and yet they knew Luke Titan was alive. They knew from his letters that he was looking forward to killing her.

Luke had never forgiven Veronica for insinuating that he'd murdered his superior in academia, although Luke *had* murdered the man. Everything that had happened in Veronica's life after that accusation could be directly attributed to Luke and the sick games he was playing with Christian.

"Luke is going to try and kill you, Ms. Lopez," Waverly had said. "The only way we can protect you is to remove you from society, or remove Veronica Lopez at least. The witness protection program will allow that to happen. It'll give you a new life and keep you from Luke's grasp."

"Aren't you trying to find him?"

"We are, and we will find him. The question you need to ask yourself is if you're willing to risk dying before that happens."

"If you kill him, can I get my life back? This one?" she had asked.

"Yes. I imagine you'll also get a nice book deal once that happens."

Veronica hated the Director for saying it, and she hated herself for liking the suggestion, as well.

In the end, she'd signed the papers because she wanted to live. It had nothing to do with a book deal, or anything else. In the end, Veronica was weak, and valued living over everything else. Over seeing her parents again. Over seeing her friends.

Even over the man she loved, Christian.

However, she couldn't take the full blame for that.

By the time she'd signed, the man she loved didn't exist any longer. Christian had changed after Lucy Speckle, but it wasn't comparable to the change he'd undergone after Luke's betrayal.

He wasn't trying to protect people, as he'd done after Speckle. Christian had quit speaking to Veronica back then because he truly didn't want her in any danger. What happened during his *Luke recovery*, as Veronica always thought of it, was entirely different. His body had healed, but his mind hadn't. His *soul* hadn't.

"I'm joining the program," she had told him at his hospital bed.

How many nights had she spent there, at his side? She couldn't count them, but each one had been agonizing, because she'd known when he was able to walk again, he would never walk with her.

Christian had stared out the window as she told him. "That's good," he'd whispered.

Tears had sprung to Veronica's eyes, and she knew he would hear them in her words, even if he couldn't see them falling down her face. "I just wanted to tell you."

"It's smart. Waverly is right. Luke will kill you if he can find you."

Veronica stood and fled the room. Those were the last words Christian had spoken to her.

Veronica lived on the West Coast now, in California. Once a bestselling author, she now worked as a senior editor at a local newspaper whose circulation was around 30,000. Her books used to sell that much in the first week of release.

Veronica still thought of herself as *Veronica*, though

everyone else knew her as Betsy Arnold. Betsy. A plain name. And Arnold? Gone was her Mexican heritage, stripped from her the same way Christian's underlying sensitivity had been.

Luke had taken everything from everyone and given nothing back.

Veronica had thought she wanted life, truly. That's why she'd signed the damned papers. It was only after she'd arrived in California to a life she didn't understand that she came to realize perhaps life wasn't that valuable after all.

Suicide. That was the thought which came to her. Always unbidden, and at the most random times. She would be sitting in front of her computer, working on a local assignment about how the lack of rainfall was impacting businesses, and the thought would suddenly arise.

You should kill yourself.

It was shocking at first, but with repetition, it came to be somewhat expected.

You should kill yourself.

When something like that is repeated enough, it starts to feel like a viable alternative.

You should kill yourself.

Veronica Lopez, now known as Betsy Arnold, had begun to give it serious consideration.

Charles led Luke Titan into the living room.

"Need anything to drink? I have sodas, beer, liquor, even water if you'd like."

Charles felt good, much better than he had yesterday when he thought about Titan in his home. He felt better because it was the day of, and not the day before. He felt better because he'd slept great last night, not to mention that all of Titan's money had been safely deposited into Charles' account.

Mostly, he felt so damn good because today people were going to die. A *lot* of them.

"No, thank you," Titan said.

Charles stopped at the living room entrance and waited for Luke to step up next to him.

"So, this is where we'll watch."

Four 50" television screens had been mounted across the walls, and Charles hadn't bothered to clean afterwards. Drywall and paint littered the hardwood floors.

"Sorry about the mess," Charles said, though he wasn't sorry at all. "I'll have to clean it up a little later. I needed space for the televisions. Each one is hooked up to the equipment in the back room. We should be able to see everything in high def as it happens."

Charles was proud of his setup. He looked at Titan to see the man's response. He was smirking, but Charles could read no more into that than he could anything else the man gave off.

"Here," Charles said, pointing at the coffee table, "I've got four two-way radios. They're all on private channels, so we'll be able to communicate to the group leaders at each site."

"What do we have at each site, Mr. Twaller?" Titan asked.

"Each group is fifty men strong, all armed with explosives and automatic weapons. They're all wearing heavy body armor, which should halt direct hits to the body. Of course, a headshot is still going to put them down. Basically, we have everything short of armored vehicles."

"How much of my armory have we used?" Titan asked.

"Around ten percent."

Titan nodded. "Well done, Mr. Twaller. I'm impressed. If you don't mind, I think I'll sit back and watch you work. I don't want an active role here."

That was the best goddamn news Charles had heard all day, and he could have kissed the son-of-a-bitch for saying it.

"Well, pull up a chair. The festivities will begin soon," Charles said, letting a smile grow across his face. "It's going to be a good time. A grand ole time!"

Charles giggled as he walked around Titan to the armchair and picked up the television remote. He flipped on the four TVs, putting each one on a different news station. The sun was up outside, and each channel had a different talking head on it. Most were discussing politics, though the third appeared to be doing a feelgood piece about a zoo somewhere.

Charles didn't care. The shooting hadn't started yet. He felt confident the zoo would disappear once the war began.

Christian hadn't gone home like Simone wanted, but he *had* gotten a better night's sleep last night. Which was odd. He should have slept poorly. Luke Titan had broken into his house and watched him sleep.

Christian should have been terrified, unable to drift off for even a second. He *was* terrified, but that hadn't hindered his sleep at all.

Is it because he's back? Christian wondered as the elevator opened on the subbasement. At four in the morning, the subbasement was empty, not even Tommy had arrived yet.

He stepped out and crossed the hallway to his office. It was humorous how they competed to get here earlier than the other to have some peace while they worked.

That was why Christian was here so dreadfully early today.

Simone swore she didn't understand why they worked such insane hours. It amused Christian when she said, "That's why Waverly hired me, I suppose. Because I'm the only sane one in this group."

Christian had come in at this time because he wanted some time alone in his mansion. He needed to know if his mind had been able to make any connections regarding what happened the previous night.

He closed the office door, then placed his bag down on his desk and sat down in his chair. The lights were on overhead, though he had a feeling it wouldn't be as bright in his mansion. It was night there, and the lights would be down because the creature that resided inside liked his rest, even if Christian wasn't sleeping all that often.

Christian sighed and closed his eyes, knowing he didn't want to see what waited for him. At least part of him didn't.

The part of himself that had slept so fully last night wanted nothing else.

CHAPTER SEVEN

Christian's mansion held an almost infinite number of rooms, and it grew larger daily. He could go to them at any time and look back on his life, remembering with infinite detail the things he'd seen and *not* seen. His mother always said that when he died, his mind should be preserved and studied to better understand how such a thing could exist.

He knew most likely that wouldn't happen. His death would be at the hands of Luke Titan, and there wouldn't be much left of his brain for the doctors to examine.

Christian wasn't concerned with the other rooms in his mansion; the ones marked *Mom,* or *The Surgeon,* or *The Priest,* or even *The Lover.* All of them were inconsequential, just like in reality. What mattered here was the top floor.

He ascended the stairs slowly. He wasn't frightened to see what waited for him. Those days had passed. There had been whole months when he couldn't go inside his mansion for fear of the things he might see.

Now, he walked slowly because he felt that he might

want to stay. To linger in Luke's remnants, the same way Luke had lingered in Christian's house the night before.

The Other spoke. "You're back."

The mirror image of Christian, they looked exactly alike except for the blood that continually leaked from the Other's eyes and mouth, and soaked his hands. He was another of Luke's remnants, although perhaps that wasn't the right term. A remnant was something old and forgotten, something left behind.

The Other was none of those things.

He was a part of Christian, but not *all* of him as Luke had hoped. Years ago, the Other had stepped out from Christian's mind, giving him advice that led to Lucy Speckle's death. That moment had nearly led to Christian murdering someone without true cause. The Other was a dangerous entity, and now he lived in Christian's mansion; he was the caretaker, and Christian could do nothing about it.

Luke may have been gone these two years, but he still held control over some things.

"Ignoring me?" the Other asked as Christian reached the last stair and arrived at the top floor.

Christian said nothing as he looked at the three statues standing at the balcony. His subconscious mind hadn't put them here. Christian had done it himself.

His mother, Veronica, and Tommy stood looking down at the massive staircase beneath them, wearing sad smiles on their faces. They didn't look at Christian, or the Other walking behind him. They stood in silence and stillness, their likenesses from before Luke got hold of them perfectly preserved in Christian's memory.

The massive floor lay behind the three statues. Christian realized that was *why* they stood here. To remind him not to get lost in Luke's memories. Regardless of the attraction that lay in Luke, if Christian remembered that Tommy could no longer stand, Christian would always return. He would always remember *what* Luke was, and *what* fate must befall him.

"What are you going to watch now?" the Other asked. "That's the only reason you come here anymore, to watch old videos of Luke like some parent who lost their child. Watching old tapes of their first few birthdays. Don't you think it's a bit sick?"

"No," Christian said as he passed the statues.

The walls lit up around him, showing him images and videos of Luke. All of them were interactions that Christian had over the years. He didn't look at them, too focused on getting to the far end of the floor. It took longer each time, as his mind built more and more space for Luke. He never knew exactly how far he'd have to walk.

"It's at least odd," the Other said.

He walked quietly next to Christian as they crossed the floor. Christian heard the blood dripping from the Other's hand. *Pitter-patter, pitter-patter* on the marble floor.

The Other may live here, but it didn't mean Christian had to speak with him.

He was right, however. Christian came here to understand more of Luke's life. A week or so after Luke had shoved a knife through Christian's cheek, he had sent a letter advising Christian to learn about his life. There had been other letters, of course, and each one gave a glimpse, although none painted the entire picture.

That was up to Christian, and his intensely gifted mind.

Sometimes there were new videos to watch, and sometimes his mind added new details to the old ones. Sometimes there was nothing at all to watch, as if his mind had lost what it once knew. That happened nowhere else in this mansion. When Christian wanted something, his mind provided it. However, this floor was different.

Finally, he and the Other reached the end of Luke's mausoleum. Two large leather chairs sat in front of an old television. It was small with rabbit ears and an odd yellow tinge to the screen that colored the videos it showed. Christian had once asked the Other why it was so different than the rest of the mansion, which used technology that outpaced what could be done in life.

"It's your home, Christian. I don't know why you do the things you do."

Christian sat in the chair on the left.

The Other remained a few feet back, not venturing forward.

"I'm getting tired of watching these," he said.

"Then don't. Feel free to disappear. Forever, if you'd like."

The *drip-drip* from behind Christian didn't stop. The Other remained quiet besides that

The video turned on, and again, Christian had no control over what it displayed. Turned out it was an oldie, but a goodie.

Luke Titan is a young boy when he first realizes the gifts bestowed upon him. Christian isn't completely sure of his age, but he knows it's before Luke is ten years old.

Christian has watched this video many times before, but each time he views it, he sees something new.

The school isn't like those built today, with massive classrooms and computers and tablets handed out to each child, regardless of their age. Christian can't be sure, but he believes this is south of the United States border. Mexico, perhaps.

Luke is sitting in the back of the class, closest to the small window. He's staring out of it with a look of longing on his face. Whatever is happening in class doesn't concern him at all. He looks similar to the man he'll grow into. The predatory nature that will one day reside beneath the mask he wears isn't there yet. He is a young boy, not the monster he will grow to be.

Christian believes that Luke wasn't born to be a murderer. He's seen too much of Luke's life to not recognize the power focal points had on him.

One of these points that would irrevocably change Luke's life is almost upon him now.

"Luke," the teacher calls from the front.

He turns his head, the longing on his face replaced by a nervousness that would one day completely disappear.

This is only the second day of school, and Luke has been passed forward for years despite his failing grades. Christian knows that the teachers in this shoddy school aren't concerned with much more than receiving their government issued paycheck. If a child doesn't want to learn, then that is on the child. It is their job to provide the information, not force feed it to their students.

For years, Luke has been allowed to stare out of the window and think his thoughts. The grades he brings home don't reflect this since the teachers do not want to deal with angry parents. As and Bs are given out like candy on Halloween. Show up at the door, and get a piece.

Until now.

This teacher wants more from him, although there's a certain sadistic nature to her reasoning. Christian cannot see directly into the teacher's thoughts, but he sees enough. If the child wants to ignore her lesson, then he will suffer for it.

"Sorry, Señorita Gomez," Luke says.

Christian hears English.

Here is the moment that Christian came to see. The place where something in Luke's mind changes forever. The focal point.

"You've been daydreaming a lot, Luke. Can you complete this problem on the board for the rest of the class?"

Snickers erupt from his classmates like tiny firecrackers. Luke doesn't look at them. He's much too nervous for that. Christian can hear the thoughts going through the boy's head. His and Luke's connection had been close two years ago, the floor in his mansion has increased it tenfold. Even time can no longer separate them.

He stares at the board. *I don't want to,* is the first thought that goes through Luke's head. It's nearly a whine, something that would never cross the mind of the man this child would grow into. *Not in front of everyone, please. Anything else. I'll stay after. I'll have detention, just don't make me go up in front of the class.*

Even at such a young age, there is grit to the boy. That determination would bloom into a force of nature later in life. Now, it's a tiny sliver of steel that runs through his spine and causes him to stand up.

The boy goes to the front of the class and looks at the math problem on the chalkboard.

The teacher stands next to him with a grin on her face that says, *You should pay attention, you little shit.*

Luke takes the chalk without looking at his teacher. He is already focusing on the math problem. It is simple for any adult, but not something Luke should know.

Christian sees a fire start inside Luke's eyes. A small light, but it's there, nonetheless.

The chalk remains at Luke's side, and Christian knows his mind is rapidly assimilating the knowledge that most children in the class haven't grasped despite trying, and some never will.

"Nine," Luke says.

The teacher stares at him without saying anything for a second, shocked he knows the answer. Christian knows from experience that she is thinking he only guessed correctly.

"Show me," she says. "Show your work on the board."

The first focal point passes, and no one in the classroom notices it. For the first time in his life, Luke understands that there's more to him than he's been told. It isn't a thought, but *knowledge*. A crystallization in his mind that no amount of brainwashing will ever change.

Math—and perhaps other disciplines—need not hold mysteries for him. He sees through its riddles with the clarity of a man holding a scoped rifle.

The next focal point is near, although he doesn't know it. He is as blind to these moments as the rest of the class. That changes nothing. The moment will come regardless of who sees it.

"No," Luke says without looking at the teacher. He doesn't know why he says it, only that he sees no reason to waste time showing something that is obvious to him.

There are other reasons, deeper ones, that he will understand as life moves forward. His disdain for those in power. His hatred for those trying to hurt him, even in small ways.

For now, he only says *no*.

The teacher is considering arguing with the boy, but she assumes what is happening. The child guessed and now is afraid his guess will be exposed. However, she must regain control of the situation since an inferior just told her no.

"Okay, Luke," she says. "Then solve this."

She snatches the chalk from his hand and scribbles out another problem across the board.

Luke stares at it. His mind is quicker this time. He absently receives the chalk from his teacher, although he doesn't raise it to the board.

"Twelve."

The teacher grabs the writing instrument again and nearly pounds the chalkboard as she writes out a problem.

"Do that one."

Luke wastes no time. "Seven-and-a-half."

Again, a problem is written. Again, the boy solves it.

This continues for a half hour with the rest of the class watching. They are unsure what is happening, but they can feel the tension filling the classroom as thick as smoke.

The math has advanced to high school level, and is nearing the point of a freshman college class. Still the boy doesn't relent. He doesn't even *slow*. His mind is expanding like a supernova, growing larger and hotter with each passing second. He's addicted now and doesn't care about the teacher or the challenge he presents to her.

He is concerned only with the knowledge on the board.

"Go sit down," the teacher finally whispers.

Luke turns to look at her for the first time. He is shocked to hear her giving up. Shocked and slightly angry, because he doesn't *want* to stop. He doesn't *want* to go sit down. He wants to continue.

"Why?" he says.

"Because I told you to." The teacher turns to the class. "Time for recess, class."

No one wastes any time and the shuffling of desks and chairs echoes in the small room.

Luke is still staring at the teacher.

"This won't be tolerated," she says. "I'm calling your mother in for a conference."

The fire inside Luke dies a quick death, smothered by the threat of parental involvement.

"Go to your desk," the teacher says. "You're not having recess today."

Luke trudges to his desk, defeated. At least, he feels that way in the moment. The truth is, two life changing events occurred in less than an hour. His mind had its first taste of the *possible.* The second, and perhaps more important, was his refusal to submit to authority and his denial when asked to show his work.

The body Luke possessed had been created years earlier, but the soul of the man was conceived that day.

"Why that scene?" the Other asked as the television screen went black.

Christian didn't turn around. He continued to stare at the TV.

"How many times have you watched it?"

Ten. Christian knew the answer, but he didn't say it. He didn't know why his mind kept going back to it, nor why he *enjoyed* it, either.

"Shall we do another? Perhaps something a little different?"

Christian looked at the yellow tinged box in front of him, the screen still dark. Would it keep going, or was that it?

The television flickered on, and Christian went back inside.

Luke thinks of the priest as "the preacher man." He knows at eleven years old how sacrilegious that is, and how severely his mother would punish him if she ever heard him say it aloud.

He won't say it where she or anyone else can hear it.

The preacher man isn't old. Luke knows he's fifty-two, and also that he makes a lot of money from his parish. From Luke's mother. From Luke and his brother, as well.

Another focal point looms close, and Luke feels this one coming. Some might blame it on the Mexican summer heat, but Luke knows better. Something is going to change, and very soon.

Every Sunday and Wednesday, Luke's mother takes him and his brother to mass. Sometimes they go twice on Sunday, attending the morning mass as well as the evening one.

Luke's mother's name is Maria Santiago. His brother's name is Mark. Neither of them know their father, and Maria never speaks of the man. The only father either boy needs is Father Marquez, also known as the preacher man.

It is time for Luke's confession. He gives confession once every six months and his mother writes down the date and time with the fervor of someone who truly believes heaven can be achieved if they work hard enough to get there. Her boys will make it to heaven if it's the last thing Maria Santiago ever does.

Some mothers want their children to attend college. Some want their children to marry well. All Maria cares about is their eternal soul, for that is most important. Colleges and marriage certificates will burn when the end of days arrives.

Christian knows all this because his mind has recreated Luke's childhood. Christian finds it odd how similar Lucy Speckle and Luke's mother were. Large differences existed, but their belief in an afterlife dominated their lives.

Luke steps into the confessional booth, and he knows the moment has arrived. He will know for the rest of his life when those few seconds that will define him approach. When he encounters them, he will meet them with a ferocity similar to his mother's—only Luke's ideas on heaven will differ wildly as the years roll on.

"Forgive me, Father, for I have sinned," Luke says once he is seated.

The preacher man is on the other side of the booth, a thin wooden screen separating them. Murder hasn't crossed Luke's mind yet, and won't for quite some time, but he does wonder why that screen is there. Is it to protect the preacher man? He smiles at that thought, given what the preacher man has done over the past decade. As far as Luke is concerned, the whole parish should have constant armed surveillance to keep the preacher man away.

"Tell me your sins, my son, and we will plead with God to forgive you."

"I've thought evil thoughts, Father."

"About who?" the preacher man asks.

"You."

A brief pause as the preacher man processes what Luke said.

"What about me?" his voice is harder, and Luke knows all he needs to.

The kindness that the man showed when Luke first sat down is only a facade. He knows as well as Luke what he's doing to the parish, and perhaps the guilt weighs heavily on him. Luke has not said a word, yet suddenly the preacher man is defensive. Maybe it's not guilt. Maybe it's fear of being discovered.

"Six months ago, I gave you five hundred pesos at confession. I found old history books in the library, Father, and the Catholic Church condemned that practice over a century ago."

The silence that comes next is longer. The preacher man is quiet and Luke thinks it's because he's trying to hold down his anger. He could be determining a response, but Luke thinks this man is far too arrogant for that. He is wondering what in the hell this kid thinks he's doing, questioning a priest.

"Libraries also have books that say the Catholic Church is evil, that all our works should be judged based on the worst actions of the worst people to ever be members. Should you listen to those books as well?"

A shot of dopamine spreads through Luke's brain at the verbal joust from the priest.

"If what the books told me matched up with my own experience, then yes. I suppose I would."

"Then you are a fool, young man. I am God's beacon and to have thoughts against me is to have thoughts against Him. Do you have your money today?"

The moment is here and Luke knows it.

"No, Father, and you will receive no more money from my family. Not from my mother or my brother. Not from me. Any money that you receive will be through alms, not through purchasing our soul for God."

"Purch—" the preacher man tries to get the word out, but he chokes on it and begins coughing. After a second, he gains control of himself. "Son, you go home to your mother and tell her to bring me a thousand pesos. Five hundred for your soul, and five hundred for the blasphemy you've committed today. If I don't have a thousand pesos by the end of the week, I'll go to her myself."

"No more money, Father," Luke says. He stands and steps outside the confessional booth. He pauses to listen on the other side of the door, wondering if the preacher man will follow him or wait for him to leave.

Luke hears no movement as he walks through the empty church.

He did well and he knows it. He spoke truth to power. Luke knows there is a God, and that such a being would never demand money in exchange for saving someone's soul. Such a being must be good, or how could He be God? The preacher man is not part of that God or His love.

Luke spoke truth to power and the preacher man will leave his family alone now.

That's what Luke thinks as he leaves the church. He would understand later that another important moment in his life had passed, and he had met it true.

His youth had been full of naiveté.

The screen turned black again and Christian came out of his trance.

The letter Luke had written about that confessional booth was spread large across the wall behind the television in digital form.

Some parts of Luke's life Christian had to piece together himself. Those were less accurate than the ones

Luke had written about. Luke had thought this one with the priest was important enough to tell Christian himself.

Dear Christian,

I am of the belief that you can fool me once, but that I'll never be fooled again. As I've grown older, the chance of someone fooling me the first time has lessened considerably, but it is still there. The chances of someone fooling me a second time is essentially zero.

God fooled me once, but never again.

I used to love God. Do you believe that? Do you find it odd that someone you consider a monster once held complete faith in the greatness of God? In the genuine goodness of him? I used to capitalize the word "him" when discussing the creature.

Life disabused me of that notion.

As these things normally go, a priest—a messenger of God— was the first to show me the truth.

My family was poor, Christian. I'm sure you've figured that out by now. We weren't poor in the American sense, where the lowest walk around with phones connected to the Internet. We were poor in the way that my brother only had one pair of pants all the way through the fourth grade. My mother hand washed them once a month in order to keep the material from wearing too thin. By the time my brother reached fifth grade, you could practically see through his pants.

That sort of poor is what I mean when I discuss my family's finances.

This priest, for the first eleven years of my life, took thousands of dollars a year from us in exchange for eternal life. We weren't special in that regard. The preacher man, as I used to call him, did this with his entire flock. He really loved us all, I suppose, to be willing to take loaves of bread from the mouths of children in order to save their souls.

Once I understood the inherent evil in this act, I could abide by it no longer. I told the preacher man the same, but like most men with power, he refused to listen. He wanted his payment every six months and was determined to get it. At least that's what he thought.

There are records of what happened to that preacher man.

My mother never paid another peso to him, but you might say my soul was damned afterward. Personally, I don't think that's true in the conventional sense of the phrase. My soul's damnation came later, if it can be damned at all. I reject the notion as God has no right to it in the first place.

I digress, although I would love to hear your thoughts on the matter. Perhaps I will one day.

Perhaps you can tell me where I went wrong, and how I ended up here, alone and intent on watching you burn.

It's in your burning that you'll reach your potential. You don't see that yet. You think your freedom, your greatest moment, will come when you look down upon my dead body. I tell you now that is false. It's in our pain when we grow, Christian. You must feel pain to finally grow into the beautiful person I know you are.

Yours,

Luke Titan, MD, PhD, Special Agent for the Federal Bureau of Investigations, Top Ten of America's Most Wanted

"How many times have you read that letter?" the Other asked.

Christian stood from the chair. He didn't know why,

exactly, but he thought he should leave his mansion now. Something was…*amiss* in the real world.

"You feel it, too?" the Other asked. "I've been thinking something was wrong for a few minutes, but I didn't want to interrupt."

CHAPTER EIGHT

Christian opened his eyes. He didn't wear a watch and didn't need to check a clock to understand the time. His mind never lost track of it. He'd been in the mansion for two hours and Tommy should be in his office by now. He would have recognized what Christian was doing when he arrived and not disturbed him.

Why do you feel like something's wrong? There's nothing out of the ordinary happening.

He still didn't know, but he didn't care. Something wasn't right.

Christian got up from his desk and walked to Tommy's office.

"Hey," he said. "Is anything going on upstairs?"

"What do you mean?"

"How long ago did you get here?"

"An hour."

Christian closed his eyes, still standing in the doorway.

"What are you doing?" Tommy asked.

Christian didn't answer. He was trying to push out any

distractions, wanting to focus on what his mind knew but couldn't tell him. *Why* did he feel so nervous? What was he missing?

It was in the air. The smell.

Christian opened his eyes. "Simone. We've got to find Simone."

Simone Goodfriend had stepped from her car about five minutes before Christian came out of his mansion. The parking lot was getting congested, but she was able to get her usual spot. Her attention wasn't on parking when the world erupted in fire around her. She was focusing on Christian, hoping that the man had gotten some sleep the night before.

She worried a lot about Christian and Tommy, even if she showed it by berating them. She had to do it like that, or else she'd be run over. The FBI wasn't inherently sexist, but crime fighting was a male profession. Simone was okay with that. A feminist, she was not, at least not in the sense that all female shortcomings could be blamed on the patriarchy.

She knew a lot of what had transpired between her two partners and Luke Titan. She had never met Titan and didn't want to, but if she did, she would be one of the first to fire a bullet at the bastard. He'd destroyed two men, two *good* men, and the world was short on those as far as Simone was concerned. At thirty-three, she was unmarried. In another life, she might have seen herself being able to settle down with someone like Christian.

Not in this life, though.

The time for settling down had passed Christian by, probably around the time Titan had plunged a knife into his face.

He needed more sleep and Tommy needed more therapy. Simone couldn't help, or rather, she couldn't help with *everything* they needed. She did what she could, and it wasn't enough. It would never be enough, not as long as Titan lived.

Simone flashed her badge at the card reader and reached for the front door when a sound like a thousand hands clapping at once erupted behind her.

She turned to see what had made the noise, her eyes wide.

White vans had surrounded the building entrance. She didn't know how many or where they'd come from, having been deep inside her mind during the walk from her car to the door, but they were here now. The "clap" had been all of the doors being slammed shut simultaneously.

Other people in the parking lot had stopped and were staring like Simone.

The vans formed a semi-circle across the parking lot. Simone's eyes followed them from one end to the other, and she briefly wondered if the other side of the building was the same.

A crazy thought, given how weird all of this was.

Men swarmed out of the front and back doors of the vans, which was when Simone realized exactly *how* weird the situation was, except weird no longer described it. Fucked was a better word.

The men wore heavy vests and each one held an automatic rifle.

A small breath escaped Simone. "RUN!" she screamed, the first sound to break out across the parking lot.

The next was the sound of bullets exploding from barrels.

* * *

"What are you talking about?" Tommy asked.

"Why isn't there an alarm going off?"

"Christian, I'm not understanding."

Christian knew he had already wasted too much time. The smell was growing stronger by the second.

"There's gunpowder in the air. Do you smell it?"

Tommy sat rigidly still as always, but his eyes flicked away from Christian to the wall.

"Oh, God," he whispered.

At that moment, an excruciatingly loud siren started booming from the walls. It wailed across the entire floor, interspersed with a calm woman's voice.

"This is not a drill. Code Nineteen. This is not a drill."

"Simone," Tommy said, his words almost completely lost in the noise around them. "She's upstairs. She probably just got to work."

Christian stopped speaking. He turned and ran, unholstering his weapon as he did. He had no idea *what* was happening, only that Luke was behind it.

He also knew that enough people had died because of Luke. Simone *wouldn't* be another casualty.

Simone hadn't done field work for the FBI, but she wasn't an idiot, either. She dove inside the building, hitting the floor with a bone-creaking slam.

The windows exploded behind her and glass flew through the air as if a tornado was roaring through the parking lot.

Simone looked up, her hair covering much of her face. The people still standing in front of her looked like deer in headlights, except they were staring at guns instead of lights. Bullets tore into them and Simone despaired as large red patches bloomed on their blue and white shirts.

The skull of a man exploded in front of her. She knew him. His name was Frederick. How many times had she talked to Frederick as she walked past security every morning?

Simone could hear nothing except for the sound of miniature explosions ripping through the air. She dropped her head to the floor and pressed her cheek to the trail of blood leaking across it. She followed its path to a fat woman who lay slumped halfway down on the floor. Her upper body was upright against the security check-in station. Her leg below her right knee was missing, the white bone and red flesh jutting out like a badly-butchered animal's.

Simone didn't cry. Her only thought to move away from the danger. Later she would find no pride in that, knowing she had been in shock.

She began to crawl.

She didn't know if people were running in behind her,

only that bullets still flew overhead. She had to get away from them. That was all that mattered.

Screams, glass, and blood filled the air as Simone crawled into the building.

"This is fun!"

Charles could barely contain himself. The first three television stations were showing live coverage of the attacks. The two-way radios sat on the coffee table, filling the room with the voices of his men and the screams of the dying. Charles didn't care about them. He was too interested in the carnage on the televisions and wondering when the last news channel would get with the program.

Aerial camera views from the helicopters flying overhead showed the parking lots. The buildings looked relatively similar, only the surrounding landscape appeared different. White vans were abandoned across the streets or parking lots, the men who had arrived in them forming loose circles around the building.

They were slowly tightening their nooses, moving in as they continued firing. Charles could *see* when the men ran out of ammunition. He watched them drop their magazines and load fresh ones with anticipation.

An explosion lit up the far left television. Someone had thrown a grenade into the building. Fire and smoke rose at the bottom of the structure.

Charles glanced over at Titan. Both men were standing almost shoulder to shoulder, although Titan stood taller than Charles.

His face held the same placid noninterest.

"What do you think?"

"This is a very good job, Mr. Twaller."

Charles nodded and looked at the man a second longer before turning back to the television screens.

It *was* a very good job, no doubt about it. This might not be the largest attack against the Federal Government in terms of death count, but it certainly was in regards to the number of attackers.

Charles forced his gaze away from the televisions and turned back to the radios. He picked up the one on the far right.

"Are any reinforcements there yet?"

The higher the elevator rose, the more Christian heard. He didn't understand what was happening, but he understood it was huge.

It sounded like a war had started.

"What are you doing?"

Christian was surprised to hear anyone inside the elevator, especially his mother. She hadn't spoken to him like this in years. None of his former apparitions showed themselves to offer him advice anymore. He had been alone, and yet here she was, standing in the corner of the elevator, ready to have a conversation.

"I'm going to help Simone," he said, knowing that he was talking to his own mind. It used to do this often, to help him make it through tough times.

"How are you going to help her, Christian? You can

shoot that gun decently at best. Do you hear what's happening through these concrete walls? How many men are up there shooting? What can you possibly be able to do?"

Christian turned away from her.

"Honey," his mother said, "I'm not trying to be cruel, but you'll die if you go through that door. Whatever is happening, one man can't stop it."

He ignored her, the same as he had the Other inside his mansion. It didn't matter what she said, nor that it might be similar to what his *actual* mother would say. He wasn't leaving Simone up there. No way.

If that meant dying, then he was okay with that. Maybe it was even preferable.

The elevator doors opened onto chaos. Christian had viewed chaos up close and with a lot at stake before. He hadn't panicked during those times, and he didn't panic now. He might never achieve the calm, almost reptilian mindset that Luke possessed at times like these, but the knowledge that he had to keep his head if Simone was to live came over him.

His gun was already raised as he looked through the smoke and shattered walls.

Christian ducked as he came out low and ran for the opposite corner. He dropped to his knees as he reached it, landing on the smooth floor and sliding until his left hand caught the corner, bringing him to a stop.

Tommy would be proud, he thought.

His mind took in everything, cataloging the dangers around him and relaying them to his conscious self with perfect timing.

Christian rose to his feet but stayed crouched as he looked around the corner. Smoke filled the air and the smell of gunpowder was heavy. The screams of the dying were everywhere, rising above the alarm's insanely loud howl.

How could he find her in here, and where in the hell was their backup?

He heard weapons discharging that lacked the heavy firepower of those outside, meaning other agents were turning outward and defending themselves.

Christian peered into the lobby, trying to see through the smoky destruction.

"You won't be able to see anything from here."

What in the hell? he wondered.

It was Dr. Michael Hanson, the psychiatrist Waverly *still* made him see. He'd never shown up as an apparition before, and yet here he was, giving advice.

Christian didn't turn around and risk getting shot. He knew these apparitions would continue speaking regardless of what he did.

"You're going to need to get out front," Hanson said.

"That's where the risk is," his mother said.

"Both of you, shut up."

They were right. Christian took off, his body bent low. He made it to the back of the security station and dropped to his ass, his back sliding down the polished wooden credenza. Bullets flew through the air above him, some smashing into the structure he was hiding behind.

It was only a matter of time before one caught him in the lung. Still kneeling, he faced the front of the building and peeked over the top.

Christian's body grew cold at the sight outside despite the war unfolding around him. His mind put the number of men approaching at around fifty. They were nearing the shattered windows and doors, mowing down everyone they saw. It was like an apocalyptic nightmare, with the healthy coming to gun down the infected.

A bullet whizzed by Christian's face. The sound of it rang in his ear after it passed. He scanned his surroundings, seeing other agents doing the same as him, only they were firing their guns, trying to hit the assailants.

"There's some cover," Hanson said with the same detachment he always used in his sessions.

"Christian, be careful," his mother said from the other side of him.

Christian dropped to his stomach and started crawling, his legs pushing him forward while he did his best to keep his gun in a firing position.

He moved out from behind the security desk's shield, avoiding the dead bodies and dying people around him. He moved past them as fast as he could, intent on finding one single person.

"*Simone!*" he shouted, hoping that she might hear his voice through the cacophony. "*Simone, can you hear me?*"

He kept scanning the room as he moved, his mind as close to a computer as any human would ever achieve as he identified and dissected every input it received.

"There," Hanson said. He was crawling, too. "Someone is moving."

Christian saw her immediately. He needed nothing else. That was Simone's red hair, and she was crawling in the wrong direction. She was heading toward the wall on the opposite side of the building.

Christian turned toward her.

Simone knew nothing except that she needed to keep moving. If she kept her body's momentum going forward, she would eventually find safety. If she stopped, she would die.

She was finally crying. Sobbing actually, but not from fear. The smoke was too much, even down on the floor. She could barely see anything, but she couldn't stop to wipe at the tears dripping down her face. That would halt her progress.

It would be her death.

Her hand touched someone's leg, sliding off a wet, meaty wound where a bullet had ripped through.

Simone pushed it out of the way, acting more on animal instinct than human. She crept, crawling, and the time felt endless, each inch a mile in her mind.

She screamed when a hand grabbed her ankle and pulled her back roughly. She stretched her hands out and kicked without looking, feeling something hard beneath her foot as she did.

The hand released her and she scurried forward, desperately wanting to get away. She'd moved forward a few feet when the hand clamped down again. This time another came immediately after, grabbing her free leg. She was pulled roughly and fast, all the way back.

"Simone, stop!"

She turned her head at the sound of the voice, and through the smoke and fear, she saw Christian.

"Stay down and follow me!"

Simone did no such thing. She reached out and hugged her troubled friend, joy surging through her.

Christian wasn't ready for the embrace, but it came with a mugger's force. Simone wrapped him in her arms and pulled him close.

They lay like lovers on the floor for a long moment.

"Okay, okay," Christian said, forcing her to let go. "We've got to go."

His voice was softer. She could hear him now she wasn't kicking him in his face. There was blood leaking from his nose but he didn't feel any pain. His adrenaline was coursing too fast.

"Come on. That way." He pointed in the opposite direction and then pushed her ahead of him, changing his mind about her following.

They crawled past the dead without sparing them a glance.

Something exploded behind them, and Simone stopped momentarily and turned around to look, but Christian shoved her, forcing her onward in a way he would have never done otherwise.

Christian didn't know where safety lay in this place, but he knew where they were going. Back to subbasement C. Back to Tommy and the small family he had in this place. If he was going to die, he'd do it there, with them.

They'd moved another fifty feet when Christian heard the sweetest sound in his life.

Heavy artillery fire from a helicopter high above.

"It's over," Luke said as the helicopter hammered the world beneath with 30mm rounds. "Few of your men will live."

"I know."

Some had fled a few minutes before, understanding that they'd overstayed their welcome.

The helicopters began arriving on all of the screens, and SWAT teams showed up in heavily armored vehicles shortly after.

The screens went black when Charles hit the off buttons on the remote controls. Luke turned and looked at the fat man.

Charles held a two-way radio to his face, and was speaking into it. "Retreat if possible. We'll be in contact." He turned the first radio off and picked up the second.

Luke wanted a drink. He left the living room and found the liquor cabinet in the kitchen easily enough. He took a glass and poured himself a double shot of Charles' eighteen-year-aged scotch. He lifted it to his nose, breathed in, and then sipped the golden liquid.

He didn't turn around when he heard the fat man waddle into the kitchen.

"What's next?"

What *was* next? That was the question he needed to answer. Luke took another sip, savoring the liquor that so much work and time had gone into creating. He wasn't drinking due to stress or sadness. It was in celebration.

He knew that the overall death count would be relatively low. Christian had been on a higher floor when Luke worked with him, and regardless, he got to work early. Even if he hadn't left the building, the chances of him being in the lobby when the attack happened were small, and outweighed by the importance of people he knew dying. Of watching people he knew die.

"Come, have one with me," he said and poured another glass. He didn't find the man pleasant, but a celebration should be shared with others. He handed the glass to Charles. "Today has been a good day and it's not yet noon. To war."

The two touched glasses and drank. "What's next?" Charles asked again.

The man was insatiable, and Luke thought he might know it. The ability to understand people's weaknesses and strengths was a rare trait. The man thought his insatiability was a strength, and right now it was.

Luke finished his drink and placed the glass down on the counter before heading to the door. "I'll need some time to review what happened today. I'll be in touch shortly."

"Hold on a goddamn second," Charles demanded. "You'll be in touch *shortly*? That's not going to work for me, friend. We just declared war on the federal government, and you going into hiding isn't good for me. The money from this attack was well and good, but I'm not keen on waiting for you while the FBI figures out who did this. We need to act fast."

Luke stopped. He had never involved someone in his actions like this before, and the reason why was right behind him. Their desires and their fears were all so petty and silly. He turned back and faced the man.

"You will be safe, as long as you took the advised precautions. We are on a timeline, Mr. Twaller, but not yours. We're on *my* timeline, and it's going to work perfectly if you act properly. So far you've shown you can, and that you're more than capable. Please do not ruin this. It would be most disappointing."

The man said nothing for a second and Luke saw he was considering a shootout right here in his home. Mr. Twaller wasn't unhinged, but he could become so if allowed. Luke would hate to kill him now. It could ruin what was to come.

"When will you be in touch?"

"Tomorrow," Luke said, holding the man's gaze like a titanium clasp.

Charles hesitated, then nodded. "Okay. Tomorrow, then."

Luke held his gaze for another second, relieved the man's moment of contemplating murder had passed.

He left the house, ready to talk to Christian.

CHAPTER NINE

Everyone in Veronica's office stood around the break room television. Veronica, or Betsy Arnold depending on who you were, had pushed her way to the front, not caring who she angered by doing so.

"What the hell is going on?" someone asked. "Is it terrorists?"

Veronica studied the TV with a combination of sick fear and fascination as the news station switched between the different attack sites. All of them were FBI buildings, and the one in Atlanta …

Tears pricked her eyes and she reached up to wipe them away. No one was looking at her, which was good, but she still had to hold it together.

It might be terrorism, but Veronica's heart said something else. It spoke two words.

Luke Titan.

Then just one, the name she'd always called him by.

Luke.

Any number of things could be happening right now,

but Veronica discarded them all. Those men on the television were well-armed and trained. If not by the military, then organizations that claimed to be. Was it a domestic terrorism attack? Not likely. The largest one had been committed by a lone wolf, Timothy McVeigh, and he hadn't gathered the kind of force this required.

This was organized. This was money in action.

This was an attack on Christian's place of work.

Luke, her heart told her again. *He's back. Two years, but he's come back.*

The thoughts ran quickly through her head as the people around her asked questions that no one could answer. Veronica pushed them from her mind, letting her logic take over. She knew very well that she would never be Christian or Luke when it came to raw brainpower, but she wasn't a slouch. She didn't need the proverbial weatherman to tell her which way the wind was blowing.

Hadn't Christian chased him? Hadn't he hounded Luke to the far ends of the Earth, traveling across continents to try and bring the man low?

Veronica had known that Luke would come back. He wouldn't be finished in America until he achieved what he wanted with Christian, but *this*? He had never operated like this before.

He was always behind the scenes, manipulating other people's psychology as much as anything else. This wasn't him in the sense of how he *preferred* to work, but he was the only person capable of this.

Luke, her heart said, bringing both fear and hope.

Fear for her life, but not of dying. Death was fine,

something she had thought much of lately, but death at Luke's hand? Veronica could lose her soul in that.

Isn't that what you're doing now? In hiding from Luke? From life? Hasn't your soul already been dying, day by day?

Yes, it had. Yes, it *was*.

His name also brought hope.

Veronica walked from the room, wiping her eyes. She didn't know if suicide was off the table, but she knew she was done hiding from Luke. If he was going to take Christian's and Tommy's souls, then why let hers die slowly while they fought with a fury she had ignored?

No. If Luke was back, she'd dare the son-of-a-bitch to come take her.

The amount of security it had taken to get Tommy and Christian to Waverly's DC office safely had lengthened their trip by an hour.

Tommy was truly impressed with the number of armed guards on every floor. He and Christian were known in Washington. They had been briefly known nationwide, and not just by their fellow FBI agents. Tommy saw respect in the eyes of the agents who recognized him, and some pity, too. He did his best to ignore it, which was easy to do with his body, but harder with his mind.

He didn't want their pity or their recognition, nor did he want their pride. He wanted them to find Luke Titan, or at the least, stop Luke from killing anyone else.

"I'm guessing neither of you have slept," Waverly said.

"No, sir," Tommy whispered.

The attack had been twenty-four hours ago, almost to the minute. Waverly had wasted no time in getting them up to DC. As soon as he'd confirmed their safety, a plane had been dispatched to pick them up.

"Don't expect to be getting any soon," the Director said. "Christian, I want you to set an appointment with Hanson today. No, don't argue about it. Just tell him I want him to clear his schedule for an hour. I can't have you losing it right now."

Tommy's eyes shifted to Christian, who had opened his mouth to protest although Waverly had cut him off.

"The nationwide body count is over two hundred already, and that's just on our side. It'll probably increase by fifty percent if we include the attackers our people took out. You two have had a day to think. Tell me, is this Luke?"

Tommy and Christian had argued for two months about their theories on Luke's plans, and Tommy's theory had won out a few days ago. The plane ride to DC had been quiet as they realized Christian had been right.

"We believe that to be the case, sir," Christian said.

Waverly stood up from the desk and walked to the glass windows that looked out from his office onto the city. He was quiet for some time, much longer than Tommy had seen before.

Tommy didn't know what to say either, and Christian was apparently at a loss for words as well.

They were in shock. Tommy knew the state well. He'd been in it for nearly a year after Luke had stabbed him through his neck. They couldn't believe what had happened yesterday.

Tommy had missed the worst of the blood and guts

pouring out across the building's lobby down in the subbasement, Christian had shoved Simone through the viscera, and Waverly had spent the last ten hours with survivors.

Still, Tommy found it hard to comprehend the destruction Luke had wreaked.

"I have to talk with the press again this morning. I don't want to give Luke credit for this, but I don't know what else to tell them," Waverly said, his back still to them. "Two hundred dead and another three hundred wounded. Fifty of them will die today. Probably another twenty tomorrow. Is this the devil? Is Luke the devil incarnate?"

Tommy had never heard Waverly say he didn't know what to do, nor heard him sound so defeated. He glanced at Christian, who was slumped back in his chair.

"What's he going to do next, Christian?" Waverly asked. "You thought he would do something like this, and he did. So what's next?"

"I don't know, sir. I haven't had time to process any of this."

"*Process?*" Waverly's voice rose as he turned around. "There's no time to fucking process, Christian? Do you think Luke is *processing*? No. He's getting ready to wipe out another few hundred of my goddamn employees, so forgive me if I need you to have already *processed*. Forgive me, Christian, if I need you to work a little faster than you are currently fucking doing."

Tommy's eyes widened as far as they could, which was only slightly. He'd heard aggression from the Director before, but not out and out insults.

"Sir," Tommy said. Waverly looked at him, the anger in

his face turning and refocusing as he did. Tommy didn't hesitate. "You want us to catch him, but what have you done since the attack occurred? As soon as we finished giving our statements, which took nearly an entire day, you put us on a plane and brought us up here. We've had barely an hour to debrief with each other, much less create any plans. We haven't been able to begin an *investigation*. I'm saying this with all due respect, sir, and you *know* I respect you, but we're going to need a few hours to get a handle on what just happened."

"A few hours? Okay, and when Luke drops a goddamn nuke on our New York office, do you think you'll need more time, or will you be ready to go then?"

Tommy wasn't backing down. "Sir, it's your job to prevent any future attacks. It's our job to find Luke. I'm asking you to let us do it."

He felt Christian's eyes on him and he *saw* Waverly's. Silence reigned in the room, but Tommy kept his gaze firm. At one point in his life, he might have been cowed by this man, but what did a glare matter when you couldn't stand up from your fucking chair?

Waverly broke the staring contest and looked down at the floor.

"A leader should apologize when he's wrong. I believe that, even if I don't always do it. You're right, Tommy. I'm sorry. I just… Goddamn it. He got you two first, and now all these other people. Folks who didn't know him, who never met him, who had goddamn *lives*."

He looked back up. "We've got to find him. We've got to neutralize him. Do you understand?"

Tommy did, and he knew Christian did as well.

Then the world exploded for the second time in less than two days when Waverly's assistant knocked on the door and walked in without waiting to be called in.

"Sir, you're going to want to see this."

It didn't take long to get on television. Veronica hadn't lost a single media contact over the past two years. Within twenty-four hours, the majority of them spent making sure she was prepared, she was back on TV. Makeup, hair, everything.

"Good evening, ladies and gentleman. I'm Brooke Yields, and this is *The War Room*. Right now, we have an exclusive interview that has a direct bearing on yesterday's attacks on the FBI. I'm sitting with Veronica Lopez. A bestselling author who became even more famous after the horrific kidnappings orchestrated by notorious ex-FBI agent, Dr. Luke Titan. Ms. Lopez disappeared from the public eye two years ago when Luke Titan became a fugitive. No one, not even her book agent knew where she went. Ms. Lopez is here today to tell her story and offer her insight into what happened yesterday."

The anchor turned from the camera and smiled at Veronica. "Thank you for coming."

"I felt I had no choice, Brooke," Veronica said, her voice grave.

"But you're here now. You haven't been heard from for the past two years. Where did you go?"

Here it was, the end of the wall of protection the FBI had built around her, wrapping so high and so tight that she couldn't see over it. She was going to destroy it all with the next sentence, and she hadn't bothered to even *call* her handler. Once she had made the decision, she'd acted.

No turning back now.

"I went into witness protection, Brooke. It was well known that Luke Titan would kill me if he knew where I was, and I felt my only option was to give up my identity and go into hiding."

"Yet, you're back? Did the FBI approve of you coming on this show?"

"They're learning of it now, just as your audience is."

The news anchor did a good job of hiding her shock, although Veronica saw her eyes widen slightly. Her mouth remained still, however, which was a good catch.

"I'm sorry," the anchor clarified. "You didn't alert the FBI that you were coming on our show? My producer told me you had."

"I lied to him, Brooke." Veronica looked off the set at Ralph, the producer she'd known for years. "Sorry, Ralph, but I knew you wouldn't bring me on if you knew I was going rogue."

"Okay," Brooke said, trying to regain control of the interview. "Nothing we can do about that now, I suppose. What made you do this? What brought you out of hiding?"

Veronica remained composed even though she knew what she said next would enrage Christian, Tommy, and Waverly. She knew that she might be jeopardizing an entire mission, but she didn't care. If Luke wanted her, he could have her.

"Luke Titan was responsible for those attacks yesterday."

There was no hiding her shock this time. "Luke Titan?" Brooke echoed. "Do you have any evidence to support this claim?"

"Not a shred, Brooke, but I know it's him. I'm putting my life at risk right now, that's how confident I am that he did this. He's after his former partners, the men he almost killed two years ago. If he wants them, then he can come get me, too."

The television was on in Luke's DC hotel room. It didn't matter which station he turned to, the news was all the same. Every channel was reporting on his war.

He'd thought it would continue that way, until he heard Veronica Lopez's voice.

"So, you're here now. You haven't been heard from for the past two years. Where did you go?"

Luke heard the news anchor ask the question and stopped ironing his suit. He placed the iron on the board and walked into the suite's living room.

There on the television was the woman he thought he'd lost. He'd spent considerable time trying to discover what had happened to her, but ultimately figured that the FBI took her underground. With more time, he might have been able to find her. There was no need now she was sitting in front of him on the television.

A smile grew on his face as he listened to her speak. He'd been ready to go see Christian. Waverly was many things, one of them being predictable. He needed to feel in control of the situation, so he would have flown Christian and Tommy in immediately.

Both were alive, Luke was sure of that. He'd watched Tommy's nurse pushing his wheelchair up the ramp as the two of them boarded their private plane.

Now, another gift. Ms. Lopez deciding she wanted a piece of Luke, too.

He watched the entire interview, imagining how angry Waverly would be when he heard about it. Luke hoped he was watching right now. Hoped his blood pressure was rising and that he'd start pressuring Christian to make some magic happen. To go deep into his mansion and find out what Luke was planning next.

"Thank you, Veronica," Luke said, smiling.

She had just made his job so much easier.

***

"You've got to be fucking kidding me," Waverly said. "This is a fucking joke, right?"

The flatscreen television on the wall showed Veronica's face. Christian hadn't seen her in years, except in his mansion. He couldn't take his gaze from her, and although Waverly was raving, Christian barely heard him.

She's so beautiful, and yet...

She's haunted. It's all through her. I might have a scar on my face, but she's got them all over her soul. You might have to stare a little harder to see them, but they're there all the same.

"Teresa, get her handler on the phone. Right now. I don't care what he's doing." Waverly didn't turn from the television as he spoke. The assistant hurried from the room, her heels pounding hard on the carpeted floor as she hustled. "What next? Luke's going to be interviewed? You think the media will put him on, too?"

No one else said anything as Veronica spoke. Fear crept over Christian as the shock of seeing his former lover dissipated. She was in danger now, as much as Tommy and Christian. Perhaps more, because what protection did she have?

"Sir, we have to send agents to her now. This show is filmed in LA, right?"

"I don't know, Christian. I don't normally go on a lot of talk shows."

"It is," Tommy said with the same fear in his voice.

The knowledge that she was dead if they did nothing chilled them both. Perhaps as soon as she walked out of the building. Christian had no idea how far Luke's hand could reach, nor how quickly.

He turned to Waverly, pushing the beautiful face on the television away for a moment. "We have to get someone to her. I'm formally requesting that someone be dispatched from our LA offices to protect her."

Waverly turned from the television. It took a second, but the anger left him.

"Okay. Listen, I've got to deal with the aftermath of this. I'll have Teresa send someone now. You two go do whatever you need to do and figure out how to catch this son-of-a-bitch. We'll meet again at five."

CHAPTER TEN

Night had fallen, and Luke felt at home with it as always. He preferred to move during the night, although it wasn't required. He could operate as easily in the daylight, but darkness reflected his true superiority.

In the light, people thought they could *see*. Some even thought they could keep up. At night, those fallacious notions disappeared. He wore the cloak of invisibility. How could anyone possibly think they could stop what they didn't see?

Finding Christian's hotel room had been easy enough. He and Tommy were traveling without protection, which was shocking and yet not surprising. They both knew the danger Luke posed, but were still operating under the presumption that Luke feared capture.

Perhaps that stemmed from the way Luke had maneuvered through their past few cases. Always behind the scenes to avoid being noticed. Or, perhaps, it stemmed from their own psychology. They were unable to shake the fact that *they* wouldn't want to be caught.

Either way, the thought that Luke would simply show up after what happened yesterday never crossed their minds.

Thus following them had been easy.

Wearing a hat and sunglasses, Luke stayed back two hundred yards at all times. He'd dressed in jeans and a plain t-shirt, looking more like a tourist than anything else.

They left the FBI office at eleven that night. Luke didn't move as he watched them exit the building. They went to the parking lot and both entered one of the handicap vans the FBI provided Tommy.

Luke's face remained still as the vehicle pulled out onto the street. The lights disappeared into the darkness and Luke stretched his arms and legs before walking down the street to his car.

The two of them were even staying at the same hotel. Their guards were absent, in part because neither had slept in a long time. They weren't thinking clearly, and Luke was counting on that.

He waited two hours, passing the time in his car. Just after one in the morning, Luke entered the hotel lobby. The bar was closed and there were two people behind the check-in desk.

Luke wore his hat, but he'd taken off his sunglasses, not wanting to worry anyone unnecessarily. After all, people wearing sunglasses in the dead of night set off alarm bells.

The young black man looked up with a smile on his face. "Hello, sir. How can I help you?"

Nice hotels hired nice employees. Luke pulled his suppressed pistol from the back of his pants and fired a single shot into the nice young man's face. He pivoted slightly and fired again, catching the female co-worker just above the bridge of her nose.

Both fell to the floor behind the counter in separate sprays of blood.

Luke walked around to the other side and bent over the man's body. His keys were attached to his belt, and Luke pulled them off, not caring about leaving fingerprints. The world knew he was back, and his visit with Christian certainly wouldn't be anonymous.

The hotel master key on the ring was a plastic card that would allow him entry to any of the guest rooms and the hotel's computer system. Luke dragged the two bodies inside a back room and shut the door as he left. He went through the computer and found Christian and Tommy's rooms with ease, then rode the elevator to their floor.

Luke went to Tommy's room first. He placed the key against the scanner and saw the green light flash. He entered the room but didn't bother closing the door softly. It shut with a *clang*.

Tommy's scent was heavy in the room and Luke breathed it in. Memories from years of work came back to him similarly to how the aroma of cooking food might remind someone of their mother.

"Christian? Anne?"

The voice was soft, like a person whispering to their lover. Luke followed it to the bedroom.

"No, Tommy. Not Christian. It's me. Who is Anne, your nurse?"

The bedroom blinds were closed and the lights off, but he could still see Tommy.

The wheelchair was next to the bed where Tommy lay

on his back, propped up to ensure that he could breathe properly throughout the night.

"I take it Anne is the woman I saw traveling with you. Did she put you into bed?"

Tommy said nothing.

"You wish you could move right now, don't you? To that gun sitting on the nightstand, which is as useless… well, as an FBI field agent without control of his limbs." Luke moved to the bed, pushing the wheelchair out of the way. He stood over Tommy. "Would you like me to turn the light on?"

No response from Tommy, but Luke turned the knob on the wall beside the bed.

Tommy squinted at Luke, then his eyes focused directly on his.

"Hey, partner," Luke said. He reached forward and touched Tommy's forehead with the back of his hand, like a mother checking a child's temperature. "How are you doing?"

Watery pools of rage filled Tommy's eyes. "I'm going to kill you. I promise."

"I'm sorry about Alice. It had to be done, though. There are bigger things at play here, Tommy. Bigger than you and me, bigger than her. It's a war that must be fought, and there will be casualties. They can't be avoided."

"Luke," Tommy whispered, his chest hitching and his voice full of desperation. "I'm going to kill you. I will watch you when you take your last breath."

"Maybe. But not tonight. Do you think of her often, Tommy? Do you think of making love to her? Do you think of holding her while you watched movies? I bet you do."

Tommy said nothing.

Luke shrugged. "Ah, well, I just wanted to say hello. I'm not done with you yet. The war is just beginning."

The former partners stared at each other for a few seconds, then Luke turned the light off and exited the hotel room in silence.

He moved briskly down the hallway and paused outside Christian's room. He would need to act quickly since Christian still had control over his body. He flashed the key against the sensor, saw green, and opened the door. Stepping inside, he moved to shut the door silently behind him, but felt the wind of someone moving close by. He raised his arms, putting his closed fists together to form an 'L' shape in front of his face like a boxer's guard.

Pain ricocheted up Luke's forearms as Christian's gun slammed into him. He made no sound, every sense focused on the next movement. The gun again swung at his head but Luke ducked, searching for his assailant.

Luke's fist snapped out like a viper, catching Christian in the stomach and causing him to bend at the waist. Another punch to Christian's nose crunched bone beneath Luke's knuckles.

His old partner was still on his feet. Luke straightened and with a god's righteousness, brought down his left fist across Christian's face.

Christian collapsed, the gun falling to the floor beside him.

Christian squeezed his eyes together. He couldn't breathe out of his nose and his face was a lake of pain. He tried to sniff, but his sinuses lit on fire.

He opened his eyes and saw a lamp on to the right illuminating the hotel room. Luke was sitting in a chair directly across from him, holding Christian's service weapon. It hung lazily from his right hand. Luke had one leg crossed over the other, looking as patient as the Buddha.

Christian realized he wasn't restrained. He sat on his chair with as much freedom to move as Luke, except for the fact that Luke had a gun and he didn't.

"I'm impressed."

Christian blinked hard, trying to shove the pain in his face away.

"How did you know I'd come?" Luke asked.

"You look like a fucking bum," Christian said as he did a once over of Luke's clothes. His ex-partner was wearing jeans and tennis shoes, clothing that didn't even exist in the stores Luke previously frequented.

"You've forced me to make adjustments, Christian. How did you know I'd come tonight?"

"I didn't. I thought it was a good probability."

"Yet you didn't tell anyone?" Luke's entire body was still, nearly a stone statue.

Christian sat opposite him with a swollen, bloodied face, his mouth open so that he could breathe.

Luke smiled. "Veronica really took a stance today, no?"

Any pain Christian felt disappeared at the mention of her name. "Fuck you."

Luke smiled. "So much anger. Have you found no peace

in the past two years? Even when you chased me to my *home* in South America, did you see me show I was disturbed? No, Christian. It's not healthy, walking around with a weight like that on your shoulders. You'll eventually end up stooped over unable to move."

"Why are you here?" Christian said.

"I wanted to palaver. I think it might be beneficial for both of us to discuss what comes next."

"You're so fucked, and you don't even know it. You attacked four FBI buildings yesterday, Luke. What do you think comes next? Whatever plans you've created, they're gone now. The body count is over two hundred. Waverly will enlist the fucking army if he needs to, but you're done. Completely."

Luke nodded and frowned slightly. He didn't look away. "That's possible, but not probable."

"Then what do you think comes next, Luke? You think you're so in control of all this, except if I was faster and stronger, you'd be dead right now."

"But you're not."

Luke stood and walked to the window, his left shoulder facing Christian so that the gun was on the other side of his body.

"Do you remember my purpose, Christian?"

"No one can forget anything that crazy."

"What is it?" Luke asked.

"Fuck you."

"There's no need for such crude language, Christian. It doesn't befit you."

"Fuck you."

Luke chuckled. "Another question, perhaps. How much

of my life do you understand? Have you seen when I was put on this quest? Do you see that I have no choice in the matter?"

"I see that you're insane, Luke. That's all. There's nothing else to you."

Luke shook his head. "You don't believe that and we both know it."

Neither of them spoke for a few seconds and Luke's words settled into Christian's mind. *We both know it.*

Christian wouldn't say anything, and he might try to fight the assertion consciously, but subconsciously? Where the truth always resided deep inside its pool? What would *it* say?

"My purpose is disorder in the face of God. You're a tool in that purpose. A very *good* tool," Luke said. "Waverly will come after me now, with more resources and focus than ever before. That's fine. It's you and I that concerns me. Where we go from here."

Christian was silent, his eyes looking at the empty chair in front of him. His mind had already gone through every possible escape scenario, but each one ended with a bullet inside him. If he sat here, he would make it out alive. Luke wasn't going to kill him. If Christian tried to run? Well, Luke might have to make more "adjustments" to his plan.

"Christian, I recognize the seriousness of what I've done. I declared war on the federal government. I intend to continue waging that war until you do what I ask of you."

"And what's that, Luke?"

"You're going to kill Veronica, Tommy, and Waverly. Your mother can live, but the rest of them have to die by your hand."

Christian's eyes widened, and for a moment complete shock kept him from doing anything else. Then, he started laughing. Loud, deep guffaws originating from deep within his chest.

"You're crazier than anyone imagined!" Christian nearly shouted the words, his face bright with pain, but he couldn't help himself. It was too funny, Luke showing up here thinking Christian might even consider his outrageous demand.

"Slow down. Think about it. You might see things my way."

Christian's laughter died as his mind focused, a single ray of intensity drilling down on Luke's words.

"There you go," Luke said without looking away from the window. "Two hundred people died yesterday. That attack was more for show than actual effectiveness. What comes next will be worse, and that's going to weigh on you, Christian. Remember how you felt when Lucy Speckle started killing people you knew? Everyone told you it was ridiculous to think you were responsible, yet you couldn't shake it. Really, that's what gave me my opening. Why that other version of yourself still lives somewhere in your head. Your guilt made you hate Lucy, and that allowed me to make you kill her."

Luke turned his head to fix Christian with a calm stare.

"Now look at where we are. We're almost the same, you and I. You're going to have to embrace my purpose as your own if you want to see your way out of this." He turned so that he faced Christian completely. "Once those three people are dead, by your hand, I'll turn myself in, Christian. How does that sound?"

Christian looked into Luke's brown eyes and he saw light in them. Not the cold, nearly dead stare that he so often gave, but something close to glee.

"We're going to kill you, Luke. That's the only *sound* I hear. You dying. Your last breaths struggling out of your caved in chest. I hear your death rattle."

"It's not my rattle you're hearing, Christian. But you'll know that soon enough."

Christian didn't look away as Luke stepped toward him.

He knew what was coming, and though fear naturally rested in him, he wouldn't give Luke the satisfaction of seeing it.

CHAPTER ELEVEN

Christian woke up, slumped in the same chair. His skull hurt, as well as his face. Luke had put him in a chokehold until…

Luke.

His eyes snapped open as everything came back to him, the fog of unconsciousness whisked away.

Christian stood up, but black spots dotted his vision and he grew lightheaded. He grabbed the chair's arm and bent over, trying to gather himself. He took two deep breaths, his eyes scanning the room as he did. He didn't see his weapon anywhere and knew Luke must have taken it.

"Tommy," he said through a nose full of snot and blood.

He straightened slowly, doing his best to keep from collapsing. Finally feeling like he had control of himself, Christian walked to the hotel door and into the hallway. He looked both ways but there was no point, Luke was gone.

Or he's with Tommy.

That sped him up. Christian ran down the hallway,

reaching Tommy's door and leaning against it. Black spots danced along his vision again; he had to focus.

You don't have a weapon, and you're going to go in there and try to save Tommy? That's your plan?

What else was there? He couldn't very well call this in. By the time anyone arrived, Tommy would be dead.

You will be, too, if you go in there now.

Christian ignored his thoughts, glad they weren't coming in the form of his mother standing in the hallway talking to him. He reached into his pocket and pulled out his wallet, then flashed Tommy's key against the scanner. The card reader flashed green and Christian stepped inside.

"Tommy!"

"In here."

Relief washed over Christian, cold but pleasant water breaking through the borderline panic which held him. He moved across the room, which was larger than his own as it was handicapped equipped. Tommy was in his bed, exactly as Christian had left him.

"He visited you, too, huh?" Tommy asked. "Looks like I got off easier."

***

Christian sat across from Michael Hanson's chair. His face was bruised and swollen like he'd gone five or six rounds in a boxing ring before being knocked out.

It was eight in the evening, and while Christian had no problem working these hours, he imagined Dr. Hanson was only here this late because the Director had told him to be.

He no longer saw Melissa. There had been no big breakup, no shouting or tears. Not even a solemn goodbye. Christian had exited the hospital and simply never gone back. There was a life before the knife went through his skull and a life after. Very few things had crossed from one side to the other. That had included many people, Melissa among them.

His relationship with Hanson was much different than the one he had shared with Melissa. Christian still wasn't sure if that was a positive or negative thing. Melissa cared. Hanson didn't. It was not that the lack of caring meant active dislike, only that what Christian decided to do didn't matter to Hanson. Either way, the man's day would continue, as would his life.

"You're probably going to want to see a doctor," Hanson said, indicating Christian's face.

"You're a doctor."

"Not the type that can help with physical injuries."

"This one was my fault," Christian said.

The psychologist looked at him for a second. Waverly had insisted Christian keep seeing him, but their distance meant the two had to communicate over the Internet. Now, thanks to Luke, they were able to meet in person.

"What do you mean?" the doctor said. "It was your fault you got beat up?"

Christian had spent the first four hours of his morning debriefing with Waverly and others as to what happened the previous night. Tommy had told the truth, Christian believed.

Himself?

No.

Not at all.

"I'm not sure I can say," Christian answered.

"Or you're not sure you want to?" Hanson asked.

Christian looked away, hurting his neck as he moved. He missed Melissa. He could have told her anything, but here? This guy was in Waverly's back pocket and he had to keep coming. Week in and week out.

"We're never going to make progress if you don't push Director Waverly from your mind, Christian. We'll keep playing these cat and mouse games. If I can be frank, I'm tired of them. I have a lot of work to do, and if you didn't notice, it's dark outside. I have a wife and a son who is getting ready to go to college, and I like eating dinner with him while I still can."

Christian said nothing.

The doctor sighed. "Okay, what do you want to talk about?"

Silence ensued. Christian stared at the window and the darkness outside.

"Chris—"

"It's my fault because I knew he was coming. I knew he'd be there. I waited for him, and I tried to attack him. Luke-*Fucking*-Titan got the upper hand and beat the shit out of me. That's why it's my fault. Because I knew he was coming and I didn't tell anyone."

A longer silence passed. Tears welled in Christian's eyes. He wasn't sure why. Anger. Rage. Frustration. All of it centered around someone he'd once loved. Confusion.

Hopelessness. Any number of feelings, all mixed together in a cesspool of depression.

"Why didn't you tell anyone?"

"Because I wanted to kill him."

Dr. Hanson paused before speaking again. "Christian, I'm truly not trying to be harsh here, but do you realize what you may have done?"

Christian nodded, a tear falling from his eye. Anger at himself, too. Perhaps even hate.

"I know you don't trust me, and perhaps you have reason not to. I must balance my duty to my patients with my duty to those that we serve, the public. It's not always an easy balance, and a problem other psychiatrists don't have to consider." He sighed. "I won't break confidentiality on this, Christian, because it might be the most honest thing you've said to me in two years."

Christian was quiet, still not looking at Hanson.

"*Others* could have captured him, if you'd alerted Waverly," the doctor said. "Do you want to stop him, Christian, or do you want to end him? There's a difference, and it's an important one."

"I don't know anymore." He flicked his gaze to meet the doctor's, the room blurry through his tears. "I know what I did. I know how many lives I may have put at risk. We could have fucking had him, right then, and right there, but I wanted to kill him…" Christian chuckled, shaking his head. "Except that's not even true. I could have killed him. I had a gun and I was able to react maybe a second before he knew I was there. I could have pulled the trigger but I tried to hit him with the gun instead."

"Why?" Hanson asked.

"I wanted to hurt him first."

The two men were silent for a few minutes, the longest Christian had sat in a shrink's office without speaking.

"Do you think you should be on this case, Christian?" Hanson asked. "Sincerely, do you think you're mentally fit for it?"

Tears still in his eyes, he said, "No."

***

Christian held the cup up for Tommy and placed the straw gently inside his mouth. Lunch had changed for Christian. Before, he'd spent his time devouring sandwiches and barely looking up to see those around him. It was humorous, when he thought about it.

He had grown colder in every area of his life, and yet at lunch, he was forced to pay close attention to Tommy. He had to serve someone else, when the rest of his time was spent serving his obsession.

He supposed he could have asked the nurse to do it, but then he'd serve no one, ever.

Christian pulled the cup back, giving him some time to swallow.

"Thanks," Tommy said. "Go ahead. Eat. I'm fine."

"You sure?" Christian asked.

"Positive."

Christian placed the cup down and sat down to unwrap one of his sandwiches. He was waiting on the call from Waverly. The one where he would say Hanson had recommended Christian be removed from Luke's case. He was, in short, waiting to be fired.

He'd said nothing to Tommy yet, and wouldn't until there wasn't any other choice.

"How's your face feeling?" Tommy asked.

"Hurts," Christian responded through a mouthful of food.

Tommy let him eat for another minute before saying, "Do you ever wonder if we can win this? If we can beat him?"

Christian looked up from his sandwich, surprised. Tommy never asked questions like that. He used to wonder if his partner ever thought them. Tommy's bone marrow was made up of both pragmatism and optimism. Questions involving "what ifs" weren't in his nature, Neither was doubting himself.

"Why are you asking that?"

Tommy wheezed a humorless laugh. "Does it sound that odd coming from me?"

Christian nodded.

"It feels odd," Tommy admitted. "I guess because I'm wondering it myself. Maybe it's because I'm sitting in a wheelchair and you have to feed me. At least Waverly gave me a nurse to wipe my ass so you wouldn't have to do it. Maybe all of that has something to do with it. Or, maybe, it's because I'm seeing the truth. He's always been too powerful. I mean, eventually everyone gets caught, I understand that. I just wonder if when he finally *is* caught, if it'll even matter by then."

Christian looked down at his sandwich, suddenly not at all hungry.

He had told no one about the deal Luke made with him. All he had to do was kill his partner, boss, and former lover, then Luke would allow himself to be captured. Christian had made up an entire story regarding their conversation, leaving out the actual words spoken.

Now Tommy was asking him if Luke could be caught.

The Other didn't show up, but Christian knew what he would have said. *Tell him that if he wants to take Luke down, all he has to do is die.*

"We'll get him," Christian said. "He's going to slip up and we'll get him when he does."

"But do you really believe that?"

Christian did, or something very close to it. Only Hanson knew that Christian had attacked Luke first. Even Luke hadn't suspected it, which meant that Christian was anticipating things that Luke couldn't see. It meant he was gaining an advantage, mentally if not physically.

However, he couldn't tell Tommy that.

Instead, he nodded and said, "I do believe it. He's not God."

No one spoke for a few seconds and Christian resumed eating out of necessity. He wouldn't have another chance to eat all day.

"I hope you're right," Tommy said. "I really do."

"She's called three times today, Christian. The last one was five minutes ago. I'm getting tired of putting her off." Simone hadn't yet flown to DC. She was working from home most days while the entire Atlanta office was shut down.

Waverly had told them this afternoon that she'd be

coming up on Thursday. Hanson hadn't told him about Christian's unfit state yet, but Waverly knew Simone would be beneficial for both Christian and Tommy.

Christian should have told him that she was doing a fine job bitching at him from Georgia, so there wasn't any need to waste taxpayer money flying her up here.

He didn't, though. He missed her, even if he wouldn't admit it.

"I need to talk to Waverly first," Christian said, referencing who kept calling him.

"No. You could have talked to him today. You've been up there for two days now, and we were all in a meeting an hour ago. You knew she'd called twice by then, and you didn't say a word."

Simone was talking about Veronica. Christian honestly didn't understand how people with less brain power than he were handling all of this. It was a whirlwind for him. Before lunch with Tommy, he'd had another meeting with Waverly, half expecting to receive his walking papers the entire time. They looked over almost twenty preliminary reports on the four buildings that had been attacked, and spent three hours combing through dossiers created on the identified attackers.

Now he had to deal with Veronica calling his office constantly.

Christian had changed his cellphone number, so she didn't have that. He'd changed his mother's too. Veronica hadn't been the reason for it. She hadn't come to mind the entire time. Yet, since she couldn't get in touch with him through her normal routes, she was annoying the hell out of Simone instead.

"She said she's heading to DC if you don't call her back. I'm not sure the Director will like her showing up at his door, ya know?" Simone asked.

Christian sighed. "You don't let up, do you?"

"When I get my way I do."

"And what is your way this time?"

"That you call the woman, Christian," she said. "Didn't you love her once? Why are you ignoring her?"

"She has an armed guard with her, Simone. It's not like I'm leaving her to the wolves."

Are you sure? Isn't that exactly what you're doing? An armed guard. That's funny. Do you think that will keep Luke from getting to her if he wants?

"We're not talking about an armed guard. We're talking about a phone call. You need to do it. I don't know everything that happened between you two, but I know that she deserves more than talking to your assistant or having me tell her I'll relay a message. Don't you think?"

"Why has every woman to ever enter my life consistently told me how wrong I am? Can I not have one who just agrees with me?"

"Maybe. When you start acting right."

Christian said goodbye and got off the phone, though he kept staring at it. He was tired and it was nearing ten at night. He wanted sleep more than anything right now. However, Simone was right. Veronica deserved more than that. A lot more.

"Then give it to her," his mother said.

She was suddenly on the bed, sitting next to Christian. She reached over and put her hand on his leg.

"You used to treat people with the love they deserved,

that they earned, even. You stopped because you thought it was better for them if you didn't show that love. Are you seeing now that it doesn't matter what you do? That you don't control the world, no matter how much you like to think you do?"

Christian stared at his feet while the figment of his imagination continued speaking.

"She's still in danger and you haven't spoken with her in years. Maybe it isn't your love that puts her in danger. Maybe it's Luke Titan."

Christian said nothing. He opened the text Simone had sent earlier containing Veronica's number and he dialed it.

"Hello?"

"Hello," Christian said, squinting as a grimace rolled across his face in anticipation of the verbal beating that would surely come.

Christian heard only silence for so long that he wondered if she'd hung up.

"Are you there?" he asked.

"Yes. It's just been a while since I've heard your voice. I was kind of taking it in."

Christian's face relaxed and he sighed. "What are you doing, Veronica? Why did you go on that goddamn television show and say all of that? You're going to get yourself killed."

"Not with the ten people you have outside my house at all times."

"It's not ten," Christian said.

"You get my point."

Christian laughed without any humor. "If it's any solace, I have about the same outside my door."

"Why?" Veronica asked.

"Well, mainly because Luke has declared war on the United States, and so far he's winning."

"That's not what I meant," Veronica said, her voice snapping off his sarcasm. "Did something happen besides what was on TV?"

Christian briefly wondered if Waverly was monitoring his cellphone, or Veronica's. Maybe the entire conversation would be recorded and listened to later. Through his exhaustion, or perhaps because of it, he decided he didn't care.

"Yeah. Luke came to visit Tommy and me."

"You're kidding," Veronica said.

"No. He tuned me up a little bit, but that was my own fault, I suppose. So now we have twenty-four hour surveillance around us both. It feels a little bit like having the Secret Service, doesn't it?"

Veronica laughed, though only briefly. "Yes, I guess it does."

A few seconds went by and then Christian said, "Why did you want me to call?"

"Isn't that obvious? I want to come out there to be with you. If he's going to kill us, Christian, we might as well be together."

Christian lay back on the hotel bed, his feet dangling off the end. He kept the phone to his ear and closed his eyes, listening to the silence between the two of them.

She didn't question if he was still there and he said nothing. Both of them knew what she was asking of him, and she had to know an answer wouldn't be immediate.

Regardless of how fast his brain worked, she wanted him to change everything he'd instilled in his life.

The walls he'd built ran so deep into the ground, and so high into the air, they couldn't be scaled or tunneled under. He was insulated, and that meant others were insulated *from* him.

Yet, the walls wouldn't stop Luke from getting to Veronica. Luke was beyond them.

No, a thought spoke, *you can stop Luke from getting to her, by killing her yourself. That's the option he's given you.*

Christian shoved the diseased idea away.

"I'll talk to Waverly tomorrow. We'll get you an escort out here," he said.

CHAPTER TWELVE

Charles had left his house and gone into hiding. He didn't want to do it, but knew he had to. The riverbeds of information were drying up for him, and quickly. He had expected a response from the FBI. Everyone involved in the operation had. But this swiftly?

No, Charles hadn't anticipated *that.*

Perhaps thinking he could somehow defeat the goddamn FBI was arrogance.

Charles was in the North Georgia Mountains. The place the abortion bombers went after blowing up unborn babies. He was in a small cabin that had a bedroom, a bathroom, and a kitchen attached to a living room. He'd arranged to stay there, and when he'd told Titan where he was heading, he'd sounded as if he couldn't care less if Charles was hiding out in hell.

The cabin was fully equipped with everything he needed to command operations. He had radio communications, burner phones, a high speed Internet connection.

The place might look like a piece of shit, but in reality, he could operate just as easily here as he could at home.

Which was all that mattered.

"Just a few more weeks of this," he said as he stared at the map on the wall. "A few more weeks, and you'll be rich and Titan will be dead."

He was looking at a state map of Alabama, focusing on Birmingham. A small, red circle encapsulated a single building. Using black, red, and green markers, Charles had traced different routes to the building. The reds were routes that wouldn't work. Blacks were better options, and green was best.

A week had passed since the attacks on the four FBI buildings. Titan had given him the task of figuring out what the next one would look like. Charles had given it some thought, and decided why try to reinvent the wheel? Hadn't Timothy McVeigh done a good bit of damage with a moving truck?

Titan had given his okay, and they were about ready to move.

Charles took the red marker from between his lips and circled one of the green routes already on the map. "That's the one."

The road contained the least amount of traffic, the fewest traffic lights, and had a direct route to the FBI building's entrance.

The FBI response would become harsher, but Charles was safe up here. The noose might be tightening, but there was still plenty of room between it and Charles' neck. The FBI was traveling up the lines of communication, trying to find the man at the top, but they were still a good way off. By the time they knew about Charles, this would be over.

He'd be rich.

Titan would be dead.

The world would be right again.

First, a lot of people needed to die.

Luke was half a mile away from the Birmingham, Alabama FBI building. He stood on top of another building. The wind blew hard so high up. He was at the roof's edge with a pair of powerful binoculars in hand. He could only see the top half of the FBI building, but it would have to do. Any closer and he'd risk danger to himself.

A few things were on Luke's mind as he waited for the building to fall. The first, and least important, was when he could rid himself of Charles Twaller. He held no doubt that the man was thinking the same thing about him. They would tolerate each other for the time being, but sooner or later, Charles would come for Luke. It was strange when he thought about it, how Charles felt himself the predator in this relationship.

Luke didn't care what the man thought, outside of *knowing* what he thought. Twaller could think he was an astronaut and it wouldn't matter. He would get no closer to killing Luke than anyone else had.

But *when* Charles Twaller died depended greatly on Christian. Twaller was magnificent at what he did, and Luke planned on increasing the pressure until Christian snapped, which meant the fat man was necessary for now.

"Will you snap, though?" Luke asked the empty rooftop. He peered through the binoculars, watching the still standing building.

Luke didn't know the answer to the question. It was the first answer he hadn't known since he was a boy in a small Mexican classroom. Christian hadn't broken yet, and it wasn't for Luke's lack of trying. This attack would be different. The FBI building was in a heavily populated area. Massive casualties would result from the attack, and all of them would be laid at Christian's feet.

He would know it, because Luke had told him how to stop this.

Luke would keep laying the dead in front of Christian, until he did what Luke commanded. The bodies would pile so high and so wide that Christian would see nothing else. No friends, no family, only the dead with their open eyes staring right back at him. Their torn apart bodies decorating his vision like Christmas ornaments on a tree.

But would he break?

Or was he too strong?

If so, that was fine. Luke's purpose would still be served, the affront to God growing greater with each death.

Yet, he wanted Christian to break. God had put Christian in Luke's way, even if Christian didn't believe it. God didn't need Christian to believe, and neither did Luke. To break Christian would be the greatest affront. To see the good bend at the knees and accept what they are, what they've become. Then God would watch Luke's creation.

The wind blew harshly against Luke's body. It was time to stop his wool gathering.

It was time to begin stacking more bodies in front of Christian.

Steven Poe was nervous as hell, and it wasn't easy to make such a man nervous. He had seen war, terrorism, and all kinds of private security ranging from diplomat escorting to out and out assassination.

Still, he knew what he was doing as he drove the van through the Birmingham streets. He'd known since he received the call two days prior. He was participating in a new kind of war.

Steven had been watching the television over the past week, as he imagined the rest of the country was. Most people were saying this type of war couldn't be defined. It wasn't terrorism. There were no political means to be gained. It wasn't warfare with another nation.

This was a private war, dictated by the whims of one man and the end goal unspecified.

The talking heads on the television were saying that the world had entered a new era. Though they were all careful not to define it, Steven knew its definition.

They had entered the Luke Titan era.

Steven had signed up for the man's army. The pay was right, which was all that mattered. The covert wars in the eighties taught Steven that flags weren't worth dying for, but money might be. Steven had decided he'd get paid good money to ruin lives when he witnessed the hell he and his colleagues created by killing dictators and creating a power vacuum.

Fifty thousand dollars to create hell on Earth simply wasn't worth it.

Steven had been contacted three days ago and the price was fair. He only had to drop this van off at the building three blocks away and he would be about ten years closer to retirement.

The plan, as it had been laid out, was simple. Security had been increased across the country, but Birmingham, Alabama—despite what they portrayed to the outside world—was still behind in most areas of life. That included FBI security.

Steven had received the credentials yesterday, and he was to show them to the security guard, then pull the van right up to the front door. The front of the building was shaped like an arrow. He would park at the crux of it, then get out and walk off.

Simple.

Once he was three or four blocks away, he would press the clicker in his pocket, sending a radio signal to the van and detonating the equivalent of four tons of dynamite.

Steven felt nervous though, regardless how simple the plan was. If something went wrong. If the credentials didn't work, or someone asked to look in the back of the van. He would either end up dead or in jail. Neither of which were great. Still, he kept a calm appearance as the vehicle rolled past the last stoplight and up to the security checkpoint.

"How are you doing?" one of the security guards asked.

Security might be lighter here than in the rest of the country, but Steven still didn't like what he saw. The guard house had three people inside it, including the person who'd stepped outside. He didn't see any automatic weapons, but everyone was packing.

"Not bad. Monday, though, ya know?" Steven said.

"Believe me, I know. Can I take a look at your identification?"

Steven pulled the two cards he'd been given from his wallet. One was a fake driver's license, the other a fake employment ID.

"One second," the man said, stepping back into the security post.

Steven placed both hands on the steering wheel and looked out the front window. The moment of truth was here. Would things go as simply as he hoped? Or would he have to shoot this man in the face, speed the van to the front, and then take off running down the street? Steven *would* do all those things, if necessary. The money was that great.

The security guard returned from the post, credentials in hand.

"Here you go, sir. If you'll pull around back, someone will be there waiting for you. If not, there's a doorbell for shipments."

"Thanks a lot."

"Not a problem."

Steven pulled the van through the gate, knowing that the security guard would be dead in about five minutes, most likely unidentifiable. His family would only know he'd died because he was at work. They wouldn't find his body, and if they did, it would be in pieces and the place he was laid to rest would contain an empty coffin.

Steven took a right instead of a left, hoping that the

security guard wasn't paying attention. He wouldn't pull the van to the back. The structural weakness rested in the front of the building and the building had to collapse *in full.*

The money was contingent on it.

He parked the vehicle and took the keys with him as he stepped out. If they did find what was in the back of this van, they wouldn't be able to move the damned thing before Steven pressed the clicker in his pocket.

There was only one entrance and exit to the premises, so Steven started walking back the way he came.

"Sir, you can't park that there," the security guard said, exiting the guard house.

"Sorry, I needed to ask you one thing. The back, it's—" Steven whipped the suppressed gun from the holster hidden by his jacket, and fired a bullet into the guard's head.

The man collapsed in a heap. Steven didn't pause. He entered the guard house and killed the other two guards before walking out.

Four blocks down the road, he pressed the button in his jacket pocket.

The wind was blowing from the east, but the blast wave surged outward from the north. Despite only being able to see the top half of the building, Luke watched the first flames rise as if hell itself had erupted.

He held the binoculars to his face, determined not to

lower them for anything. He would watch from this vantage point, just as God watched from his.

It all happened in seconds, but Luke's mind slowed it down, taking it apart piece by piece.

The blast moved upward, breaking windows as the outside pressure grew too great for their structural integrity. Internal metal rods snapped, forcing thousands of pounds of pressure onto the outside bricks, causing them to be flung into the parking lot.

A roaring fire rose from the lower floors, spreading out in all directions. Luke knew it would have been more effective to focus it only in the building's direction, but some things couldn't be helped. It blazed through the building's front doors, and although Luke couldn't see them, he knew human bodies were now burning.

Luke smiled as the building began its collapse. The heat and pressure working their lethal magic brought it down in seconds, killing everyone inside and sending a plume of shattered stone and brick into the air.

He watched for a moment longer before forcing himself to put the binoculars down. Sirens screamed as the world came to know another attack had taken place.

CHAPTER THIRTEEN

The three of them sat at a conference table, a TV mounted on the wall showing the wreckage. Everyone in the room was in shock. The sound was off, so no one could hear what the reporters were saying. There wasn't any need.

Another FBI building, just one week after the last attack. This one had been completely destroyed, brought down by a van with chemical explosives in the back.

Waverly stared at the television screen with an absence of focus that Tommy hadn't seen before.

Tommy looked at Waverly, pulling his eyes from the smoke and debris filling up the screen. The man was ghastly pale, closer to a ghost than a human.

This is personal to him, Tommy thought, and then, *Of course it is. He's at the helm and Luke is taunting him, dancing around him like a child who knows the adult is too slow to grab him.*

"Sir, we have information from the last attack," Tommy said.

Waverly didn't take his gaze from the TV. "What are we

considering the last attack? The one that happened this morning or the one that happened last week?"

"The one last week."

"Let's hear it, then."

"Local cops caught one of the mercenaries last night. He was pulled over while trying to cross the Mexican border."

Waverly looked at Tommy. "When did this come in?"

"We got it this morning. I'd been preparing to send it to you, and then this happened." Tommy's gaze flicked toward the television before coming back to the Director. "We planned on requesting to fly down and interview him."

"Go ahead. Go now." Waverly picked up the phone sitting on the conference table. He hit "1" and the line went directly to his assistant. "Get a plane ready for Tommy and Christian. They're going to need to leave within the next two hours. It's heading to?" Waverly looked at Tommy.

"El Paso, Texas."

"El Paso, Texas," the Director repeated. He hung up and looked at Christian. "You look like I feel."

"Sir," Christian said, tearing his eyes from the television for the first time since they'd sat down. "I'd like to request that Veronica comes with us."

Veronica? Tommy wondered. He knew that her desire to be with Christian had brought her to the east coast a few days ago, but why did he want her flying around on the FBI's jet with them?

You know why. He's not letting her out of his sight.

Waverly scowled. "That woman isn't as bad as Luke, but she's close. First she comes out on national TV, telling the world that Titan is responsible for mass murder. Now she's wanting to fly private on the taxpayers' dime."

Christian said nothing as he held Waverly's stare.

"I'm not going to make you give me an ultimatum, Christian," the Director said. "Go ahead and bring her along, but don't make me regret it."

"Thank you, sir."

<hr>

Tommy and Christian were riding in one car and Veronica was being brought in another. She had an FBI escort at all times now. Christian and Tommy hadn't had time to go to the hotel and pack. Waverly had sent some underlings to get what was needed, and they would meet them at the plane, the same as Veronica.

Tommy's wheelchair was in the trunk and he was sitting to the right of Christian in the back of the town car. Christian's face was still busted up, although the worst of it was behind him.

The past hour and a half had been spent learning about the man they were heading to interview. Patrick Drexler was thirty-eight years old, six-foot-two, and two hundred pounds. He had spent eight years with the army, the majority of that time as a Ranger. Once he'd retired from the military, he'd gone into private security.

He'd done two or three tours with Blackstone Consultants. The records were hazier with the private company, but they'd pinned him down as doing one tour in the middle east and one in Russia. Once he'd left Blackstone, both he and any record of him simply vanished.

Analysts were still working on finding out more information about the man, but Tommy didn't hold out much hope. Spooks like Drexler didn't drop off the map accidentally. He'd gone underground to make more money than legitimate companies like Blackstone could pay him.

They would study more on the plane. Tommy was curious to see how Christian acted around Veronica. Would he be able to focus, or was he back in a lovey-dovey state?

Tommy would have smiled if he could. The person sitting next to him didn't seem capable of that vulnerability anymore. It wasn't long ago that Christian had been asking him if he should call Veronica back after their first kiss.

The desire to smile faded as Tommy thought about the distance between the two extremes of who Christian used to be, and who he was now.

"What's bothering you?" Tommy asked. He was somewhat slumped in his seat, but that happened any time he was out of his wheelchair and sitting somewhere without the necessary restraints. It was an indignity that he had to look past.

"Besides the fact that Luke is bringing down entire buildings?" Christian asked.

"Yeah, besides that," Tommy whispered.

Christian's chuckle contained no humor. "Nothing, Tommy. That's the only thing bothering me."

"Fuck you. Don't lie to me." Tommy's whisper conveyed his anger nonetheless. "I know the story you gave Waverly is bullshit. Luke didn't break in and beat you up. I haven't said anything because I know you have your reasons, but don't think I can't see through your lies."

Tommy watched Christian stare out the window, still not saying anything. "It would help us if you told me."

Still, his partner was quiet.

"I'm not your wife, but I am probably closer to you than anyone else in this world. We've both lost a fucking lot. To keep me out of this… It's insane, Christian. What am I going to do? Run and tell Waverly what actually happened in your hotel room? Is that what you think?"

"No," Christian answered sharply.

"Then what is it?" Tommy pressed.

"Nothing, Tommy. I just need some time to think through everything that's happened."

"More bullshit," Tommy said. "When you say you need time, it means you need a few hours at most. This has been days."

Christian said nothing and Tommy gave up. He could speak until his vocal chords died completely, it wouldn't matter. Whatever had happened in that room, whatever was bothering Christian, he wasn't going to talk. At least not to Tommy. At least not yet.

What did Luke do when he wanted to know something? Tommy wondered. *The bastard set up a surveillance system inside Christian's house. He knew everything that happened, everything Christian thought. Why don't you do something similar?*

If you want to know what he's thinking, why don't you pay attention when he doesn't think you are?

It was six in the evening and the plane had landed an hour ago. The cops had transferred Drexler to the FBI building in El Paso, giving up jurisdiction willingly enough. As with the rest of the world, they wanted nothing to do with Luke.

"You're the cop Titan paralyzed?" Drexler asked. "You were all over the news for a while. It felt like I couldn't turn on the TV without seeing something about you. Now, here you are, in the flesh. Small world, I suppose."

Christian didn't react to the man in front of him, even as he taunted Tommy.

Patrick Drexler. Former military turned mercenary. Christian had learned everything he could over the past few hours about the man.

"Look," Tommy whispered. "I don't want to sit here talking to you any longer than I have to, so tell us what you know and we can move on to getting you in front of a judge."

"I asked for my lawyer six hours ago. Why isn't he here yet?" Drexler said.

"We haven't been able to get in touch with him," Christian spoke up. "Mr. Lawrence is a tough man to find."

"Yeah, I'm sure he is. Why don't you try calling the number I gave you?"

Drexler was correct. They hadn't called the phone number they'd been given, although a federal prosecutor would find it tough to prove. The IT group had used IP rerouting to "call" the lawyer's number, but the call went nowhere. A technical forensic team could figure it out, but right now, no one in the FBI gave a damn.

"We're still trying to find him. In the meantime, why don't we just talk?"

"Even by saying that, you're violating my constitutional rights, Special Agent Windsor. Don't they teach you anything about the Constitution at Quantico?"

All of it was true, but again, Christian didn't give a damn.

"Tell us who hired you and we'll get you all the lawyers you want. Hell, I imagine you'll be granted immunity if you testify. We've got a lot of leeway on our side, Patrick."

"You know, I had no idea we were working for Titan. Not until that woman started talking on television and you guys were forced to admit it. To be honest, I didn't really know what the point of the operation was, only that they were paying more than anyone else at the time."

The man spoke so freely because he knew none of this could be used against him. His rights had been violated and he could sing a tune for the next sixteen hours, detailing all the crimes he'd ever committed, and in the end, he'd walk.

"He did a number on your face. You know that? I'm surprised you survived. A knife through the skull like that…" The man shook his head. "Should have caused more damage than it did. Maybe Titan isn't so deadly after all."

Or maybe he did exactly what he wanted to, you arrogant prick, Christian thought.

"You know you can say anything and we can't use it against you. So why not just give us a name? One name and we will find a way to get you out of here. Might not be today or tomorrow, but maybe you just got pulled over for a broken taillight and no one found an M-16 sitting in your trunk."

"Aren't you military spooks supposed to be smarter than that?" Tommy asked.

The levity on the man's face died. He knew he'd fucked up by keeping that weapon on him. It had been colossally stupid because it matched up perfectly with the weapons left at the attack sites.

"I can still walk. So you tell me who's smart?" Drexler looked at Christian. "Do you think I spoke directly to whoever did the hiring? That's not how it works. There must have been three hundred men between all those sites. No one has time to individually recruit each person. I don't know who allegedly hired me. I don't care either."

Christian stood up and glanced at the camera in the corner of the room. The eye recording everything had him on record offering illegal deals to the detainee. Christian didn't care, and for once, he thought Waverly might not either. The recording would disappear because the rules were ceasing to matter. Another attack was imminent, and Christian knew it with certainty.

Luke had given him a choice, and he wasn't going to stop killing until Christian did his bidding.

"I know you've heard rumors, Patrick. *That* many people aren't hired without rumors springing up. So give us a rumor. Give me something we can use."

Drexler folded his arms. "Get me some guarantees and I'll talk. Until then, I'm not saying anything else."

Christian stared at the camera. It would do no good to threaten the man's life, and he knew it. The mercenary had made a damning mistake keeping the weapon on him, but he wasn't dumb, and he certainly wasn't scared of death.

He turned to Tommy. "Let's get him some guarantees, then."

It took another twelve hours, but the guarantees were there in front of Drexler. Christian had also given the okay to get Drexler's lawyer here. Putting papers in front of the man would do no good if he didn't have someone he trusted to tell him everything was legit.

Which it was.

It had gone all the way up to Waverly, and the details of the coverup were simple. Drexler was pulled over for a busted taillight. Undefined paraphernalia was found on his person, but his cooperation in an existing investigation would cause all charges to be dropped. Testimony in open court was not necessary. The record would be sealed and then expunged at the end of the year.

Those were the technical details.

Christian wanted a name and then this man could run to Mexico and live there forever—minus the weapon they'd found in his car. He might be a killer capable of atrocities, but he wasn't who Christian was after. He was what Lucy Speckle might term *nonessential.*

Christian was willing to let a killer go if it brought them closer to Luke.

"Everything looks good," the lawyer said. "You'll have a record, but it's sealed. In a year, it'll be gone completely." He was focusing on the documents sitting on the table before him, but he had been *pissed* when he first arrived. He knew the game Christian and the FBI had been playing, and had threatened to sue from now until the end of time.

The problem was, the weapon charge would have stuck, even if nothing Drexler said inside the interview room did.

The weapons charge was legitimate, and all the rules had been followed. So, he had to play ball if he wanted his client to get off clean.

"All right," Drexler said. "Let's not waste any more time. I'm tired."

"We all are," Tommy said, and Christian knew that was perhaps the truest thing ever spoken.

No one had slept in the past twelve hours, and it was nearing seven in the morning. Christian and Tommy were fueled by caffeine and hate, but they were quickly running out of both.

"The rumor is a man named Charles organized every-thing," Drexler told them.

"Get the fuck out of here," Tommy whispered. "If you think we're letting you go with a first name, you're even dumber than I thought."

"Just pulling your leg, my crippled friend," the merce-nary said. "Did Titan kill your sense of humor when he killed your fiancée?"

Tommy said nothing.

Good, Christian thought. *Stay strong. Fuck this guy.*

"Charles Twaller," Drexler said, his stare holding Tommy's.

"What do you know about him?"

"He's high up. I've never met him and I doubt anyone who was on the job had met him, either." There was no humor in the man's voice now. This was the trained killer that rested beneath the clown mask he had worn the rest of the day. This was the man who had gunned down inno-cents and then left before he could get what he deserved. "I've heard about him. He's a psychopath who deals in munitions; primarily transportation and storage. I've never seen him doing operations like this, so I imagine that's where Titan comes in. If Titan is behind this. I don't have any knowledge on that."

"What else do you know, Patrick?" Christian asked.

"That's it. I think Twaller may dabble in drug transportation from time to time, but I don't know much about him. I only know this because I did some research after I was contacted for the job."

"Who contacted you?" Tommy asked.

"That's not pertinent to our agreement," his lawyer said.

Drexler said nothing.

"That's the deal we cut? A name and hearsay?"

Christian liked hearing Tommy talk like this. It had been a while since he saw the man in his element. Even confined to a wheelchair, some of the old Tommy was coming out now.

"That's what you wanted," the lawyer said. "Now you have it. Is there anything else?"

"Why do you say he's a psychopath?" Christian asked, ignoring the lawyer.

"He kills drivers."

Christian was still amazed at the change in the mercenary. He was like a robot, giving out information as it was asked for, but nothing else. Charles Twaller might be a psychopath, but Christian thought one sat in front of him right now, too.

"He likes to kill the people who transport his goods. He's gotten in trouble for it before. The cartels and such don't take kindly to their men being killed, but he's skated by so far."

"What's his next attack?" Tommy interjected.

Drexler shrugged. "I don't know. I was contracted for one job and I completed it."

"Why did you take it?" Tommy asked. "Most of your colleagues died. You're the first one we were able to take alive."

"Not pertinent," the lawyer said.

Christian smiled. "Fine. This will be enough. You both can get the fuck out now."

It was one in the morning when Christian finally returned to his hotel room. He'd been able to nod off for twenty minutes earlier in the day, but other than that he hadn't slept at all.

Exhaustion wasn't a strong enough word. He wasn't sure the English language possessed one.

Veronica was up and waiting for him. Christian had made sure there were two beds available, although he wasn't going to put her in a separate room. It was too risky. Even with the FBI agents standing outside the door, he thought one more line of defense—even if it was only him —was better.

"Didn't want to risk my seduction?" Veronica said, turning the television to mute.

He hadn't been to the room yet, but knew she was talking about the separate beds.

"Sex would complicate things." In his exhaustion, he was reverting to blurting out whatever came to mind. Veronica, his mother, Melissa, and a host of other people had helped him work on it, but he just didn't care right now.

He placed his bag next to the bed and then fell onto the mattress. He turned onto his side, facing Veronica. A lamp hung on the wall between them, the light shining.

"You always knew how to woo a woman, Christian." She turned the television off and rolled onto her side. The former lovers stared at each other for a long moment before she spoke again. "Are you ready for bed?"

"I'm not sure I can sleep right now," Christian admitted.

"You look like you could sleep forever."

"I think that's called death."

"Then you look like death," she said, smiling.

Even in his current state, he couldn't help but fall in love with that smile. Every time she did it, he fell again. If only things could have been different, if only Luke had never existed.

Then you wouldn't even know her.

"Are we safe for the night?" she asked.

Christian nodded. "As safe as we can be. There are two guards outside our door. Two outside Tommy's. I did consider putting the three of us in one room."

He didn't smile, but she chuckled lightly, knowing he was kidding.

The two stared at each other for a few minutes without speaking, yet no awkwardness fell across them. Christian watched as her eyes slowly started closing. She was falling asleep, almost unaware, and with no self-conscious desire to hide it.

After everything, she still felt safe with him. She still felt at home. Christian couldn't help but feel thankful. They would never be together again, but it still felt good to be loved. To know that even though he'd pushed everyone away by creating that massive wall around himself, people still cared.

How much do you care about her? Enough to let the world burn down around you? Enough to let everyone else in it die? Because that's what you're doing.

Christian hadn't fallen asleep because he knew he couldn't. Not yet. He needed to go inside his mansion, tired or not. Sleep was for those that could afford it, and Christian couldn't right now. He had not thought about Luke's edict for the most part. The day had demanded his full attention. Every day demanded it. But each one brought more terror and disorder created by Luke.

Now, in the silence of the hotel room, he could go into himself and see what he was missing. The rest of the day had been spent focusing on this Charles Twaller man. He was not a ghost, but publicly he was nothing like the mercenary had described.

"He's too clean," Tommy had said. "No one is this clean when someone like Drexler mentions their name."

Christian closed his eyes and felt sleep trying to push his consciousness out of the way, wanting to drag him down into its dark depths for an unknown amount of time. He shoved the urge aside roughly, turning his intense focus to what needed to be done.

While others would have fallen asleep without a thought, Christian's mind overpowered his body's will.

CHAPTER FOURTEEN

"Every time I see you, you look worse."

The Other's eyes were bleeding, dark red blood dripping down his face. It slid down his neck and dripped off the point of his chin, but he looked at Christian as if he didn't notice.

Christian breezed by him. He hadn't come to chat. He wanted to look at Luke's past again. The more he thought about it, the more he believed the answers lay there. He thought Luke wanted him to know it, too. Why else had Luke brought his past up so much? Why had he put so much weight on it?

"You're probably right. If something is hidden, it's in there. Something that makes the man tick."

Christian ignored the Other and continued walking to the back of the floor. He didn't look at any of the walls or other memorabilia that had been set up over the years. Regardless of how hard he shoved sleep away, he desperately wanted it, and only this last thing kept him from it.

He found the chair and television where he'd last left them.

The Other had moved to stand in front of the TV. Blood splattered on the floor beneath him. "What do you think it'll show today?"

"I don't know," Christian said. "Move out of the way." He took his seat and the Other did as he was told, leaving a line of sight to the television.

It wasted no time, sensing Christian's need. It flashed on and Christian fell into Luke's history.

The preacher man, as Luke thinks of him, is sitting with Luke's mother.

Luke is outside. He knows why the preacher man has come. He is here to ensure that Luke never again says such things to him, and never again threatens to interrupt his cash flow.

He won't frame it like that to Luke's mother. He will speak in terms of the Lord, and eternal souls. He'll mention the devil and angels. He'll cloak the whole conversation with the Bible, draping its pages over his message like a protective shield.

Luke knows all this, and still, he lets the preacher man do his talking.

Luke has made up his mind about the priest, although he cannot tell his mother. When she calls him inside the house, if the preacher man is still there, he will take his chastisement in silence.

His mother is his world. Her, and his brother. They are

all he has. All he knows as truth. While his mind is still expanding at an astronomical speed, he has yet to learn what lies outside his small world. For now, all that matters is his tiny family. He will not disrespect his mother, not even in front of the preacher man.

"Luke, will you come here, please?"

Luke feels a brief flare of anger try to rise, but he knows it won't serve him so he discards it. He *doesn't* understand how special that ability is, especially for someone as young as he is. Emotions drive the rest of the world, but at eleven, Luke is coming to master his own.

He turns from the broken porch and pulls back the screen door, entering. The house is not a large place. His mother and the preacher man are sitting in the kitchen/living room. There are two bedrooms attached to this main room, one for Luke and his brother, the other for his mother.

"Father Marquez told me about your last confession, Luke."

Luke nods without looking at the preacher man. His eyes are on his mother.

"What do you have to say for yourself?"

Luke isn't at the place yet where he refuses to lie. That comes later in his life. He would have lied to God himself if it would save his mother pain, and so he says, "I'm sorry."

His mother looks at him hard for a few seconds. "Are you?"

"Yes. I shouldn't have said that. I am sorry." He turns to the preacher man. "I'm sorry, Father Marquez. I will not speak to you like that again."

"Son, I worry about you," the preacher man says. "When

you say such things to me, I wonder if perhaps the devil has undue influence over you. Your mother worries, too."

Luke doesn't know if the preacher man is using his mother as someone might use a sword, cutting through Luke's attack and defenses, or if the preacher man is simply talking. If it is the former, then the priest surely knows Luke is lying and has no intention of keeping quiet in the future. If it is the latter, then the preacher man is stupid.

"I know." Luke turns back to his mom. "I'm sorry. I promise to be more respectful."

"What made you talk like that to him?"

Two focal points would take place this day, and the first had arrived. Luke had lied once, but now he needed to say something that would resonate with people. He needed to say something convincing enough to allow his mother to continue living her life without fear of what might be happening to her son, as well as to ensure the preacher man worries no more about his cash flow.

In short, Luke needs to read and react to people in a way that allows him to continue moving through the world undisturbed.

Christian understands that this is a trait successful sociopaths possess, although to classify Luke as a sociopath would be a gross oversimplification.

Like everything else in Luke's young life, he flies past the focal point without any hindrance.

"I saw your budget, Mom. You left it out on the table and you know I'm good with numbers. I saw how much we were spending on the church."

"Honey," his mother said, reaching out to touch his knee. "You don't need to worry about any of that. That's my job. I make sure we have enough money each month, and part of being good Christians is making sure we give to God what is His."

She looked back at the priest, but she didn't remove her hand from Luke's knee. "I'm sorry, Father. He's a good boy. He just wants to make sure we're okay. I promise you, nothing like this will happen again."

Luke looks at the preacher man, too. "I promise as well, Father. I'm very sorry."

Luke is alone in his room and the night is upon him. He's already starting to enjoy both being alone and the darkness. He doesn't know why yet, but it feels like home. His brother sleeps next to him, but Luke is alone with his thoughts since his brother is unconscious. In the future, he will learn that he can be even *more* alone, but in such small spaces, this is all he knows.

He is thinking about the preacher man. About how he came to Luke's house and disturbed his mother.

Luke can allow a lot to happen in life. Indeed, he already has. Slights come and go in their small town, especially when they live in such poverty. None of them are consequential to Luke.

Except for this.

The preacher man does not see *him* as a man at all. He thinks that bypassing Luke is as simple as showing up at his house and talking with his mother. He thinks that the payments will continue despite Luke deciding before his confession that would no longer happen.

So, the preacher man and Luke are at odds.

There are a multitude of things that Luke can do to prove to the priest that he is foolish and has severely underestimated Luke's dedication to his family. The problem is, Luke doesn't know which one to choose.

Luke's mind is rushing through the possibilities, and he watches with fascination as it takes each option and follows a path to its most logical conclusion. He has done this before, but not with something as serious as he is considering.

The crux is does he want to scare the priest, or does he want to end the priest? The fact that he so easily considers murder is lost on him. It simply makes sense. If something is against him, then it should be ended. If it is against his family, then it must be ended.

Christian watches these thought processes with a sense of awe. For years, he had lived next to someone who had first contemplated murder with ease at a very, very young age. Yet, he had not noticed it, not until it was too late.

Luke reaches his conclusion in the early morning hours. He has thought on this longer than he will most of his other decisions. The sticking point being whether it was smarter to murder the priest, or just scare the man.

Luke doesn't know it as he rolls over to sleep, but he will regret this single decision for the rest of his life.

Three days have passed since the preacher man came to Luke's house.

Now, Luke is at the preacher man's house.

He is leaning against a tree on the street outside of the cathedral, staring at the closed doors as the sun peeks over the horizon.

Luke is young and doesn't understand the error in his strategy. He will very soon. His natural inclination is to attack hard and leave no doubt that he is the superior in any struggle. That is his plan this morning, and while he will leave no sign that he is responsible, the preacher man is smart enough to understand.

Enough time has been spent watching. Luke crosses the street. The church doors are unlocked. He quietly opens the one on the right and slips inside. He has yet to learn how to move without making sound, although he already walks as if he is nearly weightless.

The cathedral is silent. The priest is still asleep. Luke had been counting on the man not waking early for prayers or meditation. He was a false priest, an imposter who collected his money no differently than the Mexican gangs that run many of the neighborhoods.

There is always someone to pay, always someone who wants to harm Luke's family. Perhaps he will deal with the gangs once this preacher man is taken care of, but the largest portion of his family's budget is dedicated to this mockery of God.

Luke walks through the cathedral, paying no attention to the empty pews. He heads to the statue of Christ on the cross. Luke kneels before it.

"I'm sorry, Lord. I do not mean any disrespect, but I think you know that."

He keeps his head lowered for a few more seconds, hoping that his prayers are heard. He understands the nature of this attack, and the very real possibility that his soul will be damned. He must hope that the Lord understands it is for a bigger cause, for a *holy* cause. For his family.

His prayers finished, Luke stands and walks onto the chancel, where the fake plants stand to the right. There is imitation straw inside the pots, and he knows this will be flammable. Luke's mind has figured out all the necessary details over the past few days, most of the time without any active input from him.

It is, both for Luke in the past and Christian now, a remarkable thing to witness.

Luke pulls a lighter from his right pocket and a tiny bottle from his left. It contains no more than eight ounces, but they are a potent eight.

He douses the false straw with lighter fluid, then pauses and looks at the church's organ to his left. Using the bottle, he draws a line to it. From there, he circles around the back of the chancel, behind the cross, and ends on the other side of the room.

He heads back to the fake plants, his movements eerie in their silence.

Luke flicks the small lighter in his hand and brings it close to the plant. The fire ignites almost immediately and he steps back. He watches it rise up the plastic plant's flammable coating.

The fire crawls out of the pot and spills to the floor. From there, the race is on. It follows the half circle Luke created, and the interior of the church is quickly ablaze.

It's in this moment that Luke decides to wait. He hadn't planned to leave any evidence, but he can't help himself.

The arrogance that he would show later in life first reveals itself in this cathedral.

He steps down from the chancel, the smoke growing as the fire spreads. He walks to the front of the church, pausing in front of the doors and waits.

The fire alarm starts its siren, and Luke waits. Sweat erupts from his forehead. The room is heating up and the smoke is becoming thicker and darker.

Still, Luke waits.

Finally, the preacher man emerges. He's naked except for underwear, his fat stomach protruding further than his dick could ever hope.

He's staring at the fire, but Luke's eyes never leave him. The priest turns for the door, hoping to make it out of this alive. He sees Luke. Their eyes meet for a single second, and then Luke turns and walks out, leaving the priest to deal with the fire.

His message is clear.

He would come to realize, albeit too late, that he needed to create much clearer messages in the future.

The screen went blank and Christian stood from his chair.

Why that one? Why is it progressing chronologically again? There's more to his life, so why is it focusing on the beginning?

He glared at the Other, but his bloody eyes only stared back. No answer was forthcoming.

"You never shut up, and now you've got nothing."

"This is your mind, Christian. Answer your own questions," the Other said.

Christian turned away and looked back at the maze showing the time he had spent with Luke. Answers lay there, too, but not the ones that Christian needed. Those answers had brought Christian to Luke's truth, but what he needed was something to take him to Luke's future.

Christian crossed the floor, heeding none of it. He took the long stairs down and wound his way to a much smaller room. Above the door, the name *Charles Twaller* was inscribed. Christian opened it and stepped inside. His mind had created this place from today's research. He wasn't getting anywhere with the television upstairs, so maybe finding Twaller would at least slow the carnage.

That's all Christian could hope for right now. To stop all the death.

"You could give some consideration to his offer," the Other said, reappearing outside the door.

It wasn't even a possibility. Christian had told no one, and he wasn't going to, either. Tommy might have known he lied to Waverly about what happened. Hell, he might even know what had happened, even if his guess was unconfirmed, but Christian wasn't going to tell him the option Luke had given him.

He wouldn't entertain it, but the FBI would. They'd watch Christian around the clock if they knew the ultimatum, destroying any possibility of his effectiveness.

"You never think you'll do what Luke wants, but somehow, you always do. Remember the Lover? You almost killed him. Did you think that was possible in the beginning?"

"Just shut up," Christian snapped.

The room in front of him held what he knew about

Charles Twaller's life. It wasn't much, but his mind was filling in the missing pieces. Twaller hadn't been poor when he was younger. Not in any real sense of the word. But he had looked around and seen nothing but rich people, which made him feel poor.

That's what drove Twaller. The accumulation of wealth. It stemmed from his parents being middle class in an upper class town.

Christian felt certain the man had been born about as close to psychopathy as possible. No one could say for certain whether nature or nurture controlled *everything*. Still, it was possible to accumulate wealth and not kill people while doing it. Luke had picked a near perfect person for this job; a *smart* psychopath, and one that knew how to hide.

That was the biggest problem with Twaller. He was almost completely hidden. His life was a blank slate. Records showed him as owning some laundromats up north, and that was all.

Christian moved his hand through the air, as if shooing a fly. The screen built into the wall flashed to life, displaying a map with three green lights on it. These were the only three spots where anything amiss occurred when it came to Twaller.

Drexler hadn't been lying. Drivers did come up missing around Twaller. However, there wasn't any way to pin the missing people to Twaller. There was no real reason to suspect he had anything to do with them at all. The only connection was what Christian figured out earlier that day. Charles Twaller had been in the same town at the same time that these three people had gone missing.

Their names weren't important. They were extremely low level operators. What mattered was that they'd been murdered for no reason. Christian believed those murders had happened at Twaller's hand.

He was smart and organized, but also unwieldy at times. In some ways, he was like the other killers Christian had chased in what felt like a previous lifetime.

The map on the wall zoomed in on Georgia, the green and black lines of roads replaced with a satellite vision.

"Is he here? In Georgia?" Christian said aloud.

Where?

CHAPTER FIFTEEN

Charles opened the cabin door. The security cameras had showed him who was coming while his visitor was still a mile away. Even so, he was surprised to see him, and Charles didn't like surprises. He was used to schedules and appointments, not people who showed up unannounced on his doorstep.

And it's you I'll come for, he thought, his mind settling.

Eventually, he would come for Luke Titan, making all of these indignities worth it.

"Nice of you to show up. Unannounced," Charles said.

"It couldn't be helped," Titan answered.

Charles stared up at the man, then stepped back and allowed him to enter.

Titan stepped through the door and entered the sparse living room. He turned around slowly, taking it in.

"It's not as nice as I'm used to, as you can see," Charles said.

"You've certainly made a lot of sacrifices for our endeavor."

Charles heard the sarcasm underlying the words, but said nothing. He didn't have time for Titan's jabs. They held no interest for him anymore. The man may have been the smartest person to ever live, but he'd be dead soon enough. All those brains wouldn't make a whit of difference when he was underneath six feet of dirt.

"The building came down nicely," Titan said.

"Yes, but we may have a problem."

"With?"

"I think one of the men we used got picked up in Texas. He may have talked."

"He probably did. Does he know your name?" Titan asked.

"I'm sure most people in the operation know who was setting it up. The people I choose are smart and have been around a while. They'll have a network that will leak my name eventually."

"Do you have a contingency plan?"

"Of course. That's partly why I'm up here in these goddamn woods."

"Well, we needn't worry then," Titan said.

"Sure, no need to worry." Twaller walked past Titan and went to the refrigerator. He pulled out a Diet Dr. Pepper and popped the lid on the can, tilting it up to his mouth. He finished his sip, and looked at Titan. "So, what's next? I think we might have another three attacks left, and then we'll have to quit. The heat will be too much by then. It may already be too much."

Titan didn't turn around to look at Twaller. "No, we're not going to quit, Mr. Twaller. We're going to push this until we're both dead, or until something happens on the other side."

Charles swallowed, his throat suddenly dry despite the soda. He didn't know what this psycho was talking about, but he had no intention of dying during this operation. "Excuse me?"

"There's no way we're stopping at five." Titan turned his gaze fully on Charles. "We're in this until we die or an old friend of mine gives me what I want."

"Just what the fuck is that?" Charles asked. His hand was tightening on the soda can, though he hadn't bent the aluminum yet.

Luke cocked his head and Charles thought he was deciding whether to answer him.

"I suppose it can't hurt," Titan said. "Christian Windsor, you know his name, correct?"

"Your old partner."

"That's right. Well, we will quit when he kills everyone close to him. Otherwise, we keep going."

Charles stared, unable to find words. All of them, every single one in the English language, had flown from his brain like birds leaving for winter. This man was insane. So far beyond insane that he wasn't classifiable, or even certifiable. He was simply *beyond*. Here they were, waging war against the United States government, and his condition for surrender was an old friend killing his own family.

"Are you wondering what you've gotten yourself into, Mr. Twaller?"

Charles said nothing. He didn't notice his lower lip was slightly open, giving him the look of a huge fish staring dumbly through the walls of a fish tank.

"I'm an idealist," Titan said. "I'm not in this for money. I'm in this for purpose. You can, if you choose, leave, but there will be consequences. We have an agreement, and if you break it, I will be forced to take action given the amount of capital I've invested in you."

Charles recognized he was being threatened, but still, he couldn't find any goddamn words. The man's face held him captive, unable to break free of its trance.

"Onward and upward, am I right?" Titan asked.

Charles closed his eyes, trying to block out the man's stare. A few seconds passed, both standing in silence, and then he opened his eyes.

"No," he said. "No, you psychotic fuck. I'm not dying for this cause of yours. I'm not doing another goddamn thing, do you understand *that*? This is over, *am I fucking right?*"

Charles turned, intent on grabbing the gun that sat just on the other side of the refrigerator. He moved two feet, and was reaching for it, when he felt iron grips on his shoulders.

He let out a high squeal like a pig being stuck with a poker as he was lifted off his feet. No one, not since Charles beat up that fucking kid in grade school, had laid hands on him.

As he was flying through the air, his only thought as the world passed him by was, *the fucking indignity.*

He hit the ground, slid across the floor, and slammed into the wall. The picture frames above fell, breaking on the floor around him. He looked up and saw a demon in the room with him. A demon who moved faster than any human to ever exist, who may as well have been the devil himself.

By the time Charles recovered from the shock, the demon was nearly on top of him. Titan's face held no anger or hate. It was still, like the water of an undisturbed pond. He was at peace as he reached down and took hold of Charles' collar.

Charles was suddenly moving upward. The man's strength was greater than he had imagined. He let out another squeal as he was lifted from the floor to above Titan's head.

"Do you want to kill me, Mr. Twaller?" Titan asked, not an ounce of strain showing in his voice. "Do you want to get that gun and put a bullet through my face?"

Charles squealed again, wanting to be put down. To not be touched. To get *the fuck* away from the man.

"Go ahead, Mr. Twaller. Get the gun."

The demon dropped him, and all at once, Charles was standing on his own two feet. Titan was a safe distance away, looking unruffled as if he hadn't just thrown him across the cabin.

Pain radiated across the back of Charles' head, but he made no motion to touch it. He didn't move at all.

"The gun is waiting, Mr. Twaller. Pick it up and shoot me, if you dare. Rid yourself of me."

Charles didn't move. Fear froze him in place with that same stupid expression of a fish stuck in an aquarium of ice.

"No? You don't want to? This will be your last chance," Titan told him. "If you do not kill me now, you will never, ever, get this opportunity again."

Charles couldn't move. He could barely think. He was

in shock at being handled in such a fashion, not to mention the demon's face. How he'd done it all so calmly.

"Okay, Mr. Twaller, then we will move past my murder." Titan glanced at the cuffs of his shirt, and put them both into place. "I'm ready for our next attack, and I have a good idea of how it should go."

Tommy and Veronica were sitting at the small breakfast table next to the window in his hotel room. Veronica had helped him set up his computer so that he could work at night from here. The three of them were still in El Paso. They were supposed to leave tomorrow. Another day had passed since talking with Drexler, and Christian had spent most of it alone inside his mansion.

Veronica had knocked on Tommy's door hours ago.

"Christian needs space," she'd said, and that had been all that was needed.

Tommy invited her in. Veronica had brought her computer, and after she set up Tommy's station, she opened hers.

"Have a lot of work?" he whispered.

"Yes, actually. The emails haven't stopped since I went on that television show."

"What do they want, the people emailing you?"

"Ha! Don't you already have access?" she said.

"I'm sure someone in the FBI does, but Christian and I certainly aren't monitoring them."

"A lot of emails are from old friends that I had to cut

off. Book deals. Old relationships in publishing. Job offers. A *lot* of job offers."

"You going to take any of them?" Tommy asked.

Veronica shrugged. "I'm going to try to live through the day. That's all I can do."

"You're probably right," Tommy said. "As sad as that is."

They passed a lot of the time in silence. Tommy was focusing on Charles Twaller, reading through reports that came in. An all-points bulletin had been put out on him, with instructions to keep it out of the press. They didn't want to spook him, causing him to go farther underground. A man with enough power to keep his record this clean could disappear for a long time.

"How are you, Tommy?" Veronica asked, breaking him from his concentration.

"I'm okay," he said as he glanced up from the screen.

She laughed, weakly and without mirth. "Yeah, everyone involved with this is okay. Christian is. I am. Waverly is. And *you* certainly *are*."

He knew what she meant, but he also knew why he didn't ever venture down that path. He couldn't. He'd never find his way back out.

"You don't have to talk about it, Tommy. I just want you to tell me how you're feeling. That's all. A few words." She tilted the top of her laptop down, giving her a clear view of Tommy. "I can't talk to Christian about this. He's in his own world. I hate to say it, but the man I loved, he's not there anymore. I still love him, but that's only because I can't stop."

There were tears in her eyes. "I have no one I can talk to

about this, Tommy. No one but you. I'm asking you to just talk to me for a minute."

A cold, reptilian thought came to Tommy. *What would Luke do?*

An answer, just as chilly, came immediately. *He would talk to her. He would set up cameras throughout Christian's house so he knew what was happening all the time. Here is your camera, Tommy. Right in front of you. So open up, talk to her. Have her watch Christian for you.*

A part of him hated what he was thinking, but then an image of Alice sitting at a kitchen table with a hole in her head and blood covering her face came to him and it dashed the hatred into innumerable pieces.

"What do you want to know?" Tommy asked, pushing the image of her unseeing eyes from his mind and focusing on the woman in front of him.

"I don't know," Veronica said. "Just what you're feeling. How you've been."

Tommy's chest hitched once, the closest he could come to a laugh these days. "I mean, I get by. I don't think about it much, to be honest. If I stopped and thought about everything that had happened, I'm not sure I could keep going. I wouldn't want to."

Veronica nodded. "That's the way I felt. Clearly, what happened to me wasn't nearly like what happened to you, but I often wondered whether going into hiding was worth it? Was life worth all of that?"

"Is it?" Tommy said.

"Is it for you?"

He looked away. "It depends on if I think about every-thing that happened. If I think about Alice, about what I lost… Fuck, about what *she* lost, and how she lost it." He met her stare. "Then no, it's not worth it. The pain becomes too great. It turns into a cloud, Veronica. One bigger than an atomic bomb creates. Its blackness blots out the rest of the world. The rest of the universe, even. I see nothing else but it rushing right for me. If I think too long, that cloud will rush *over* me, and there'll be nothing left."

Tears were in his eyes, blurring his vision. He couldn't stop them, and he didn't want to. They gave realism to what he said, creating intimacy. He knew his honesty would help with what he needed later.

Tommy's chest hitched again, his broken laugh coming out in a rasp. "I can't even clean my own face. Hell, no. It's not worth it."

Veronica stood from her side of the table and walked to him. Using one thumb, she wiped the right side of his face, and then the left, clearing the tears. She leaned forward and kissed his forehead. "I'm so sorry, Tommy."

Tommy's emotion had been real, but he knew the truth. He had set her up to be used later.

Am I any different from Luke? he wondered.

Christian was close to making a connection. He could feel it.

Maps were pinned across every wall inside Charles Twaller's room inside Christian's head. He thought Twaller was most likely in Georgia, the reason being Luke's visit. Luke had been able to come to Christian's home while he slept, before the first attack.

If Twaller was commanding the operation, then that meant Luke would have been in close proximity. So, they had orchestrated the catastrophe from Georgia... But where, and where had they gone afterward?

Property records showed nothing in Charles Twaller's name. Not in Georgia, anyway.

Men were already sitting outside of his offices in Pennsylvania, but everything appeared to be closed down. The judge had denied them a warrant, saying hearsay from a questionable source didn't meet the burden of proof.

Luke burned down the church when the priest disobeyed him. Now, he's burning down the United States. There's a buffer separating him and the actual warfare. Charles Twaller.

Christian turned away from the maps. He was missing something, but he could feel he was nearly upon it.

What did Luke love? What had caused him to burn down the church?

His mother and brother. His family.

Almost there.

Would Charles Twaller love his family?

Except he had none.

"Not under *that* name," the Other said.

Christian's mind came to rest and the screens on the walls around him went blank.

No, *Charles Twaller* had no family, but if one wanted to protect them, what would one do? Especially in a business such as his. Would he keep his name? Or would that allow people easy access to his family, to those he cared about?

"We're looking for the wrong person," Christian said.

CHAPTER SIXTEEN

Charles Twaller wasn't concerned with his name any more than he was how many polar bears had been eradicated by global warming. He was concerned with Luke Titan, and growing more so by the minute.

The psycho had left the cabin, and as soon as he did, Charles had made a call. Two bodyguards were on their way now. That would be the last time Titan put his hands on Charles, and in all likelihood, the last time the two of them ever spoke in person.

Because the next time Titan showed up, Charles' bodyguards would be under instructions to shoot him right in the fucking face.

He was fuming, although the dollar figures Titan had spoken about before leaving helped alleviate his rage. It was a hell of a lot of money, and half had already been deposited. The other half would come once the operation was completed.

When that money was in its place, Charles would be finished with this whole enterprise. Titan wanted him to keep going until he either died or some ex-fucking-toy of his went on a killing spree? Thanks, but no thanks, babe. Charles was done with all of it.

So far, they had killed around four hundred people, and leveled one building. What Titan wanted to do next would eclipse all of that.

"It'll be harder to get," Charles told him.

"The cost of that difficulty has been added to your payment," Titan responded.

Which was true.

"Can you do it?" Titan had asked.

"Yeah, I should be able to."

Charles hadn't trafficked in this before. The penalties were far more severe than guns. He had, however, been offered jobs involving it, but he always turned them down.

The connections were still there. Charles could utilize them.

"Do you want to?" the fat man wondered aloud, alone in his cabin.

For the first time, the answer that came back was *no*. It wasn't that he held no interest in watching this new weapon work on people. He was *intensely* interested in that. Charles didn't want to work with Titan anymore. He didn't want anything to do with the psychopath.

The money.

Always the money.

One more score and then Titan died.

Charles had already agreed to find the weapon. Maybe that part would be fun. He had always wanted to see what sarin gas could do.

"He changed his name in 1998."

Tommy had been poring through records for the past two hours. He knew he could have a junior agent working on this, but it was too important to outsource. He and Christian needed to take the lead on this, because if they were mistaken, or didn't find the correct name, Twaller wouldn't be found.

"You're sure?"

Christian paced the narrow aisle of the plane taking them back to DC. Veronica sat to the back left of the private plane. Tommy faced her diagonally. Christian had remained seated for the first three minutes of the flight, but even with the fasten seatbelt lights still on, he'd unbuckled and stood up and started pacing.

"Christian, you're gonna hurt yourself!" Veronica had said.

Christian had said nothing back to her, although he'd absently rubbed the pink scar on his cheek with his thumb. Maybe he didn't know he was doing it, or maybe he was saying, *Not too worried about it, dear*. Either way, he didn't sit down.

"I'm as sure as I can be," Tommy said, answering his question. "I think these records were purposefully buried. Maybe someone was paid to make them nearly impossible to find. You can't seal these things, at least not without meeting very specific criteria. But you can make them harder to dig up."

"How so?" Christian said.

"You move the records around. I think the name change

took place in Philadelphia, but I found it in Tucson, Arizona."

"How is that even possible?" Veronica asked.

"It's easier when you're using older documents. Most of this was done on paper, not digitally. So, you simply pay a mailroom clerk to find the document and ship it somewhere else. You do that twelve times, and that creates a trail that can barely be followed."

"He shipped his name change document twelve separate times?" Christian asked.

"That's what I'm seeing."

"But how did *you* find it?" Veronica said.

"The document wasn't ever scanned, but the case number was entered. I followed that."

"Do you have the name?" Christian asked.

"No, they never scanned the actual document. It's sitting in the lower court's archive."

Christian stopped pacing and walked to the front of the plane. He knocked on the pilot's door.

"Yes, sir?" the pilot said as he opened it.

"We're going to Tucson, Arizona. We need to make it before the court closes for the day."

"Did you find it?" Charles asked his assistant.

"Yes."

"When can we have it by?"

"That depends on how much you want to pay."

"Price doesn't matter."

"Three days."

"Okay," Charles said. "Get it."

He hung up the phone, knowing his assistant would do as he said. The procurement hadn't been hard, but Charles hadn't expected it to be. Weapons were available if you had the money to buy them. Charles imagined it had always been so, all the way back to primitive man. The cost for weapons had been different then. Early man paid with physical labor as he carved his sticks or found his stones, but all the same, weapons were available for those who wanted them.

Charles had more work to complete. Work just as important as procuring the gas.

He needed to pick a target.

None of what Titan was doing was *new*. Gunning people down and blowing up buildings had been done by every two-bit terrorist to ever exist. Charles knew the man was smart, but if he was being honest, he was more impressed with Titan's ruthlessness. The way he had moved across the cabin's living room like a lithe predatory cat reminded Charles of himself somewhat.

Charles hated the man, but he couldn't deny the attractiveness of such an instinct to kill.

What came next? Perhaps this was the real difference between Titan and the other terrorists who bombed Europe every other week. They killed indiscriminately, but not Titan.

His target was very specific this time, and it was Charles' job to ensure compliance.

Charles waddled to the couch and took his laptop from the coffee table. His stomach didn't leave a lot of room to set it on his legs, but no matter. His knees would work fine.

He was using Tor, the encrypted browser that ensured his searches were private. He was safe as he started typing in keywords. Which was good. Necessary, even. What Charles was looking up would trigger bots throughout the federal government. Algorithms that would see his search parameters and then begin their searches on *him*.

No need to worry.

"FBI buildings with onsite childcare" wouldn't be picked up by anything, bot or human.

Christian sat in the hotel lobby. Night had fallen outside. Other than the random hotel guest, he was alone. The staff were somewhere around, although Christian hadn't seen them in a few minutes.

They had the name. Charles Twaller had been born Randy McStein.

Charles Twaller might not have any family, but Randy did. He had an eighty-three year-old mother who lived in Boston. Rebecca McStein. Her husband was deceased, but she had a daughter and Randy a sister. Alicia McStein.

A whole, regular family.

Did they know about Randy's name change? Did they know about his job? Did he send them money every month, playing the dutiful son and brother? Did he treat them well while gunning down innocents? While blowing up buildings?

Christian didn't know, but he was going to find out.

"Hey," Veronica said as she rolled her suitcase across the

lobby. She held a cup of coffee in her free hand. "Want me to get you a cup?"

Christian saw how exhausted she looked, but they had no other choice. This was his life, and she'd asked to join it. She'd stepped out of the shadows and insisted that he take her along. "I'll get one."

"You see Tommy on the way down?" he asked.

"I stopped by his room. I think he's ready for you. I can go get his things if you want to be alone a little longer."

"No, I will. Do you think you can talk to me for a second?" He looked down at his shoes, feeling uncomfortable at asking something so bold. So much of his life had changed. Yet when it came to Veronica, he still felt like a child.

"Sure." She took a seat across from him.

"I, um… I don't know how to say this, to be honest."

"Then just say it."

But he couldn't do that, and he knew it. He hadn't told anyone, and had been debating for days whether he should let Veronica know. In the end, it came down to her life. Tommy and Waverly mattered, but they'd signed up knowing death was a possibility. Perhaps an argument could be made that Veronica had too, given how many times she kept coming back. But still, her involvement was not the same as the other two.

Christian was resolute in his refusal to pay any heed to Luke's ultimatum. Insanity. A million people could die and still Christian wouldn't raise a hand to the three people Luke said he had to kill.

Yet, another, more cynical part of him said he might not

have a choice in the end. Luke might have his way regardless of Christian's feelings on the subject.

"Christian?" Veronica asked.

He looked up, realizing he'd been lost in thought.

"Sorry." He wanted to look at the floor, but he kept his eyes on her. "I'm going to tell you something, and you can't tell anyone else. Not Tommy. Not anyone. Okay?"

Concern crossed her face. "Okay, Christian. You know I won't."

"Except, there might come a time when you *have* to tell them." His eyes broke the gaze and went to his shoes. He smiled at the contradiction in his statement. "If you think I'm going to do it, then you have to tell Tommy."

"What are you talking about?"

"When Luke broke into my hotel room, he told me something, Veronica. I haven't repeated this to anyone else. I can't, because I'll be taken off the case." He sighed. "He said that he'll stop all this if I kill you, Waverly, and Tommy. He said he'd turn himself in."

Christian could feel her eyes on him. Her silence said more than words could. She understood how insane it sounded, how *Luke* it sounded. Maybe she understood why he was telling her, too. Because Luke had a way of making the impossible, possible. A way of turning virgins into whores and saints into killers.

"I'm not going to do it. It doesn't matter what *he* does. But..." He trailed off, unsure how to finish the sentence.

"You don't know what might happen."

"Right," he said. That was the politest way to say that more time with Luke pulling the strings could make something that sounded insane now sound like a perfectly reasonable solution. "I'm going to go get Tommy."

Christian stood and said nothing else before leaving the lobby to get his partner.

They boarded the plane along with the nurse, Anne. Tommy barely noticed her. He wheeled himself to his usual place, across from Christian and diagonal to Veronica.

He was glad to be sitting diagonally from her during the flight. He wanted to watch her, because something had happened. Tommy should have been concerned that they were headed to Charles Twaller's family, or *Randy's*. He wasn't.

Tommy was concerned with Veronica. He'd seen her thirty minutes before they boarded the van that had taken them to the jet, and she'd been normal. As normal as someone could be when flying around the country looking into a killer's past, anyway.

When he saw her again on the ride over, that normality had been replaced with fear that radiated from her like poison from a dirty bomb.

He was quiet during the ride over, but he spoke up as she sat down inside the plane.

"You okay, Veronica?"

Her eyes darted around as if she wasn't completely sure where she was. As though his voice had woken her from a deep slumber, and it was taking a moment to reorient herself.

"Yeah, Tommy, I'm okay. I'm just tired." She smiled at

him and he knew she was lying. Was it Luke or Christian? Someone had gotten to her and the smile said he would get it out of her. She thought they were connected in a way that couldn't be duplicated with others. Both victims of Luke, and horribly so.

Perhaps she was right in that.

She was wrong as well. Tommy was a victim, but he was different than most. Some victims wanted to be left alone to retreat and deal with their pain. Not Tommy. He wanted vengeance.

Whatever Christian was hiding... Tommy thought it could give him his vengeance.

CHAPTER SEVENTEEN

Rebecca McStein looked at Christian and Tommy as though they were bugs to be squashed. Not bugs to be feared, but insects that were an annoyance rather than those that could harm anyone. You simply stepped on them, then swept them up for disposal.

"Ma'am," Christian tried again, "We would like to speak to your son. Have you had any contact with him lately?"

The woman didn't respond. She glared at them as though she hadn't heard the question. This had been going on for the past few minutes. Christian glanced at Tommy.

"She doesn't seem like she wants to speak with us, does she?" Tommy said, his eyes remaining on the uncooperative woman. "Mrs. McStein, do you know how we could reach your son? Randy, or Charles, if that's what you call him now."

Christian didn't think this was the first time law enforcement agents had arrived at her door asking questions about her offspring. No flicker of recognition or fear showed in her eyes at the mention of his two separate names. The woman was a rock.

"Your daughter, then," Christian asked, "is she still at 911 Rainbow Road?"

Finally, he'd hit a nerve. The corners of her eyes squeezed together slightly, and her otherwise placid lips tightened.

"Alicia, right?" Tommy asked. "That's her name?"

"Don't you bother my daughter with any of this," the woman said, her first words since admitting her name.

"We don't want to, Mrs. McStein, but you're not being very helpful right now," Tommy whispered. "We're trying to discuss your son with you, but you're staring at us like we're speaking a different language."

"Alicia hasn't done anything wrong, so you just stay away from her."

"May we come in, then?" Christian asked.

"You have a warrant?"

Christian said nothing.

"No, I didn't think so," the old lady said. "No, you can't come in. Don't come back, either. Not unless you have a warrant. And stay away from my daughter, you understand?"

Christian smiled, his lip curling into a sneer. "We'll be heading over there next, Mrs. McStein. You have a great day."

The woman stared for a second longer, fire nearly erupting from her irises. Christian and Tommy both matched her stare, until she finally shut the door in their faces.

"Well, if her son is half as much of an asshole as she is, it makes sense why he'd be working with Luke." Tommy turned his wheelchair and started back down the walkway to the rental car.

Christian walked faster to catch up. "Are we heading to speak to the daughter now?"

"We didn't fly to Boston to leave empty handed."

"Do you think we can get a warrant for her phone line? She's probably going to call him right now."

"You know the answer to that," Tommy said. "No judge is giving us a warrant with the non-existent evidence in our possession."

Christian knew he was right. He was asking in the hope that Tommy might say something different. He helped Tommy into the van before loading the wheelchair into the back. He then went around to the driver's seat and climbed inside.

Tommy was quiet as Christian input coordinates for the daughter's home into the GPS, then started the vehicle and pulled out on the street.

A few minutes passed before Tommy said, "Did you notice something different about Veronica during the flight?"

"What do you mean?" Christian said.

"She seemed off, like something was bothering her."

Something was. Christian had been given an ultimatum, to either kill her and the rest of his friends, or the attacks would continue. Christian had told her not to tell Tommy. He hadn't said a word about keeping her demeanor the same.

"No, I don't think so," Christian said. He didn't like lying to Tommy, no more than he already had.

"Are you sure?"

Christian looked at the passenger's side. "Huh?"

"I just mean, did she say anything to you that I should know about? We're all in this together, for better or worse. If it's something that's going to affect us, then I'd like to know."

It affects you, Tommy, but I can't tell you that. I can't tell you anything about it, because to do so would mean I couldn't chase Luke anymore.

"Not that I know of," he said.

Neither spoke again as they drove across town. Christian didn't know what Tommy was thinking, and he didn't like that at all. He and Tommy were usually in sync, but no longer.

He suspects. And why shouldn't he? He knows you lied about what happened in the hotel room. Maybe he knows you're lying about Veronica, too.

What did it matter? Whatever Tommy was thinking, it wouldn't change Christian's decision. Hell, the *reason* he'd told Veronica was so that she could pull the emergency lever and tell Tommy if need be. There were safeguards in place now, so Tommy's worry—or mistrust—was misplaced. Christian had taken care of it.

What could he do in a wheelchair? Christian hated thinking that, but it was reality. Tommy couldn't stop Christian short of shooting him. There would be no showdown on the street like there had been at Hanson's house. No chokehold that brought Christian to the ground.

His mother spoke from the backseat. "You didn't used to think like this."

Didn't you always say I have it in me to be more flexible in my thinking, Mom? Christian thought.

"Here we are." Christian brought the van to a stop with Tommy's side facing opposite the house. Neither spoke about it, but watching Christian move a crippled agent into his wheelchair wouldn't strike fear into the heart of the woman they'd come to see. While it was something Christian didn't like considering, it was necessary.

A car sat in the driveway. Since it was Saturday, Christian was hopeful the woman was here. If not, they'd have to wait.

Christian stepped from the van and went to the opposite side to help Tommy into his wheelchair. Once Tommy was situated, the two started up the driveway.

"Let's hope she's better than the mother," Tommy whispered.

Christian smiled slightly but said nothing. He rang the doorbell and the two waited.

No one came.

He rang the bell again.

They heard footsteps inside, then the door was opened by a relatively young woman. She was tall and thin, looking very different from the mother and the pictures they had seen of the brother.

Christian thought the woman pretty. She looked worried, which was a good thing. Very different from the mother's reaction.

"She told me you two were coming," the woman said. "I'm Alicia." She didn't look at them as she spoke, but up at the sky above. "It looks like it's going to rain. You'd better come on in and we can talk inside." She stepped back and opened the door wider. "Do you need me to open the garage door? Would that be easier for you to get your wheelchair in?"

She spoke like someone who had been on a meth binge for the past three days, each word rapidly firing out in an attempt to keep up with her mind. Christian didn't think drugs were involved. Despite the woman's sad face, she appeared healthy enough.

"No, thank you, ma'am," Tommy said. "We should be able to manage. Thank you for inviting us in. I think we should introduce ourselves first."

"No need. Mom already told me who you are." Her voice changed, mimicking that of the old witch they'd met earlier. "The bastard in the wheelchair says he is Phillips, and the bastard standing up is Windsor. Don't let them in."

Christian's eyes widened and he smiled. "Well, her memory is good, at least."

"That might be the only thing good about her," Alicia McStein said. "Come on in before it pours."

***

It took an hour for Charles' mother to reach him. She'd had to call multiple people and wait on multiple callbacks, but she had no choice. No one did when they were trying to reach the man formerly known as Randy McStein.

Charles knew his mother would always think of him by that name. His birth name.

"Randy, the police just left. They're going to your sister's now."

"Alicia?"

"Do you have any other sisters that I'm not aware of?" his mother asked.

"Are they the police, Mom, or are they the FBI?"

"FBI."

"You're sure?"

"Do you think I'm a fool, Randy? How many years have I been answering doors to cops? I listen when they speak and then, somehow despite my ever increasing age, I remember what they say. These two were FBI."

The old bat was annoying, but if Charles loved anyone, it was his mother. He didn't know it, but the feelings he held for her resembled Christian's relationship with his mother.

"Thanks, Mom. What is Alicia going to tell them?"

"Who can tell? She might give them your address if she knows it."

She didn't, but his mother wasn't too far off. Alicia didn't approve of her brother's activities, or at least those she knew about. She probably would have turned him in without being asked if she'd known *everything*.

"Okay. I'll take care of it."

"You'd better. I'm tired of people showing up on my doorstep asking questions."

Never mind that no one had showed up on her doorstep in over a decade. She wasn't letting go of anything, ever.

"Okay, Mom. Talk to you later. Love you."

Charles hung up and looked out across the cabin.

The FBI had his name, both his current and former one. They couldn't get to him, so they were going after his family. His mother was solid, but his sister? What would she say?

Charles didn't know. She hadn't been in this position before. If they told her what he was suspected of, Charles didn't know what she would do.

The next operation was nearly ready to commence. Charles was prepared to call Titan and let him know the details, but now *this* had been placed in his lap.

He realized he'd forgotten to ask his mother something important. He picked the phone back up and dialed her number, his side encrypting the conversation before the phone began ringing.

"McStein residence," his mother answered as if they were still in the fifties.

"Mom, it's me. Do you remember their names? The FBI guys?"

"One was Windsor, the other was Phillips. Phillips was in a wheelchair. Windsor had a scar on his face."

"Thanks, Mom."

He hung up for the second time. He'd recognized the names at once. Titan's old partners. One of them could end this whole business by killing a few people. Instead, they were getting close to Charles.

He wasn't worried about them finding him immediately. Flying out of the country would be tougher now, but not impossible. He had multiple identities he could use, but he didn't like those fuckers putting pressure on his family. He didn't want them showing up at his mother's doorstep as if she had anything to do with this.

And it's you I'll come for, he thought, the old lyric rolling through his mind again.

So he would. He wouldn't tell Titan a word about his intentions, either. That might be the best way to go about this whole thing. Steal Titan's victory by killing his partners, take his money, and then kill him when he realized it was all too late.

Charles started giggling.

God, this was too good to be true.

"Randy is… He's different than anyone else I know," Alicia McStein said.

"How so?" Tommy asked.

"The rest of the world. You and I, Special Agent Windsor, we all live by certain moral norms. My brother doesn't. He never has. I don't think he's done all the horrible things that my mother claims he's done, but I know that he hasn't lived like a saint."

"Your mother says he's done horrible things?" Christian asked. "She seemed to be in his corner when we stopped by."

"Oh, she is. She definitely is. That doesn't mean she won't bitch about him, though. If Mom does anything well, it's bitch." Alicia laughed without the least bit of self-consciousness.

"Well, Ms. McStein, we need to speak with your brother. He's not in any trouble yet, but we have reason to believe he's involved in some pretty serious offenses."

"Like?"

Tommy's whisper had the feel of a small breeze moving through a cemetery. "The four FBI building attacks, as well as the one that was blown up last week."

The smile on Alicia's face died. She said nothing for a second, and then, "You're not kidding, are you? You think he had something to do with that?"

"Yes, ma'am, we do," Christian said.

Alicia sat forward and broke eye contact, looking across her living room.

Christian knew from the dossier that she lived alone and had no kids. She kept the house clean and appeared to be someone who had her life in order, regardless of what the rest of her family was like.

"Why do you think that? I've been watching the news. I know who you both are. The people on the broadcast don't stop talking about you two, do you know that? You're almost celebrities." She laughed again, without the previous humor.

"No, ma'am. We haven't been watching a lot of television," Tommy whispered.

"Why would he be involved in this?" she asked.

"Because Luke Titan hired him. We think Luke has been planning something like this for quite some time. To do this, he had to amass an arsenal, and that's where your brother comes in. Do you know what his business is?"

"Not exactly."

Christian took over, knowing the effort it took for Tommy to speak. "He is an arms trafficker. He moves them across the country, and across the world. He stores them and sells them, but that was it up until now. We believe Luke Titan enticed your brother to join him, and he's using his connections to execute Luke's vision."

Alicia shook her head, struggling to assimilate the information he had given her.

Christian recognized that he'd called Luke by his first name. He shouldn't do that in front of other people. It personalized the man too much and would make whoever they spoke with feel Christian and Tommy might be close to him.

"Ms. McStein," he continued. "I hope you can see how important it is that we speak to him immediately. We could be mistaken, in which case your brother could help clarify that. But if we're not wrong, a lot more people may die if we can't find him."

She looked away again, still shaking her head. Christian couldn't tell if it was in disbelief, or if she was telling them she wouldn't help.

Long moments of silence passed.

"I would help, if I could," she said finally. "But I can't. I haven't spoken to Randy in years. We were never that close, like I said, he was a…different person. I know that he loves me the best he can, and I love him. Even so, I never liked being around him all that much. It seemed like he was always trying to find an angle to work." She looked up. "My mother still talks to him. I'm sure of it. She can get you in touch with him."

"That doesn't seem very likely, given our first meeting."

Another humorless chuckle. "Probably right, but if anyone in our family can get you to Randy, it's her. I'm sorry, I wish I could be of more help, but I really can't. I imagine my mom's already called him. He already knows you're here."

"You think so?" Tommy said.

She nodded. "My mom bitches, but she's close to him. He's her only son. If you guys came here looking for him, then he knows it by now."

By the time Christian and Tommy were leaving Alicia McStein's house, Charles was already finalizing his plans.

The sarin gas attack would still happen. That was necessary to keep Titan satisfied for the next week or so. Charles was concerned with *after* the attack, because that's when things would get fun for *him*.

Two men were being dispatched. They would reach his mother's house within five hours. They weren't going to contact his mom. They were going to find the two FBI agents who were digging too deeply. Charles didn't blame them. Their organization was under attack, after all. However, consequence didn't always follow blame. Sometimes consequence simply followed, regardless of who was at fault.

The two men had instructions. To watch and follow Windsor and Phillips and ensure that they didn't drop out of sight.

With that taken care of, Charles needed to give Titan a call and let him know the plans he was privy to. Charles had been careful when making his *other* arrangements. He had underestimated Titan when he'd reached for the gun inside the cabin, intent on killing him right then. He wouldn't underestimate the man again.

The phone rang once and then that eerie, calm voice was on the line.

"Hello, Mr. Twaller."

"Hey. We're ready."

"Good. Do you have a target?"

"That's what I wanted to talk to you about. There are quite a few daycares across this great land of ours, but I think there's a unique opportunity with one."

"Which one is that?" Titan asked.

"DC."

Silence came over the line. It stretched on for so long that Charles pulled the phone away from his ear to see if the call was still connected. As he put it back to his ear, he heard the man on the other end laughing.

"Yes, Mr. Twaller," he said through cold chuckles. "That's perfect. Just perfect."

CHAPTER EIGHTEEN

Christian lay in his bed with the lights off. Veronica was asleep in the bed next to his, and had been for a few hours. Christian couldn't sleep. He imagined Tommy was dealing with the same problem.

Waverly had dispersed teams of agents to watch Charles/Randy's mother's house and was working back channels to find a friendly judge who would issue a warrant. Now it was a waiting game. They had returned to the hotel, eaten dinner, then retreated to their rooms. He and Veronica had talked for a little while.

Christian thought what she knew was weighing heavily on her mind. She was scared of him, even if she wouldn't come out and say it. She was scared of what he might do.

Are you not? he wondered.

No, strangely enough. What Luke wanted him to do was just so far beyond the realm of possibility that it didn't matter.

Then why did you tell her? Why did you say she should tell Tommy, if the time ever came to do so?

Christian sighed and rolled over, turning his back to Veronica. He wasn't going to kill her or anyone else besides Luke, and even that would be a stretch.

He felt his phone vibrating next to him on the bed. Who would be calling him this late? Waverly? Christian reached for the phone and immediately saw the number was blocked. Heavy cold like a lead vest blanketed his whole body.

Only one person would call him with a blocked number.

Christian sat up, still holding the phone. He looked across the room at Veronica, her face toward him, her mouth slightly open.

Christian put the phone to his ear. "Hello," he said in a low voice.

"Hi, Christian," Luke's voice was clear.

"Where are you?" Christian asked.

"I'm not close by. I'm attending to other things right now. Judging by how quietly you're speaking, I think you have Ms. Lopez with you. How is that relationship working?"

Christian swallowed, still looking at Veronica. The cold wouldn't dissipate and goosebumps rose on his skin. "Why are you calling, Luke?"

"I wanted to see if you've thought any more about what I proposed the last time we spoke. Are you willing to kill her yet?"

"You know the answer to that is no."

"I suppose I do, but I wanted to give you another chance. Do you remember what I told you before I stabbed you in the face?"

Christian did. He remembered everything perfectly until the blackness swarmed him as the pain and blood loss became too heavy for his mind to keep going.

"I said that if you wanted to kill me, that would be your only chance. That if you waited any longer, it would grow much harder to do so. You remember that, right?"

Silence from Christian.

"I'm telling you something similar now, but with a difference. If you want to keep your sanity, kill her now. After tomorrow, it's going to be much harder to hold on to that sanity. Am I right? Is she there with you?"

Christian looked away from Veronica, somehow frightened that Luke might be able to see her through his eyes.

"She is. Kill her, Christian. For your own sake. End her life, then go to Tommy's room and do the same to him. You'll be doing him a favor, and you know it. When you're finished, I'll come get you. We can leave, Christian. You and me. We'll never be caught."

Christian's eyes slid back to Veronica, unable to help it. A part of him—a part he would never admit existed to anyone—*wanted* that. To go with Luke, to spend the rest of his days with the only person who'd ever understood him.

Christian swallowed and closed his eyes. "No, Luke."

"You're sure? After tomorrow, things are going to change."

"Where are you?" Christian said.

"I wanted to give you the option. I'm always looking out for you, even if you don't think that's the case."

Christian said nothing.

"Good night, my old friend."

The line went dead.

Christian didn't sleep for the rest of the night. He woke Waverly and Tommy, telling them both about the threat for tomorrow. He left out the parts of the conversation that held no bearing on the impending attack.

Alerts went out across the FBI, but in the end, neither Christian nor the FBI's warning made any difference.

Director Alan Waverly arrived at work early, just as he had each day for the past twenty years. He took a different route than most other employees. He parked on a different deck and took an elevator that very few people had access to. In the beginning, at least, he was safe.

It was the parking decks that were the problem, the ones that Waverly didn't visit. More specifically, it was the cars that went into the decks. Charles Twaller's sly genius showed itself in that move. He had realized that the most perfect delivery mechanism were the people themselves.

Sarin has a much higher potency than cyanide, and the ability to easily turn from its natural liquid form into a gas. Charles had wracked his brain for a long time to understand how he could take sarin from the outside and deliver it *inside*.

The eureka moment had come at an inopportune time, but who can control when genius strikes? He had been lying in bed, the darkness of the mountains surrounding him. He was dozing when it hit him, sleep just about to wash over with its peaceful necessity.

The cars, he thought. *The cars. No one checks them, not if you have a badge. The driver flashes the badge at a reader, perhaps waves at the guard on duty, and then they're safe. It would take too much time to check each car for weapons, chemical or otherwise.*

He didn't sleep at all the rest of the night.

By the time morning arrived, everything had been worked out. He only needed to operationalize the strategy, and that wouldn't be hard. Resources were poured into learning who worked at the FBI's DC building, and then more poured into learning where those people *lived*.

The timing was what mattered. His men went out the night before to over four hundred employees' homes. As Luke was speaking to Christian over the phone, Twaller's people were working. No one was arrested.

Out of more than four hundred employees, one hundred and fifty vehicles were located. Not a high percentage, but a high percentage was not needed.

The canisters were attached beneath the cars, a small and simple technology. A timer was built into each one and programmed to release the gas at a set time the next morning.

Cars rolled through the parking decks at the north and south entrances. Some of the cars arrived early, some late, but that was the beauty of the plan. At 7:50AM, the canisters began releasing their poison. Sarin is odorless, tasteless, and invisible to the eye. The gas moved like oxygen, spraying throughout the parking decks. It filled level after level, and the people heading to work walked right through it, breathing it in and collecting it on their clothes.

Sarin gas can continue releasing from strands of clothing for up to thirty minutes. The canisters had been the initial method of delivery, but the second and most important phase of the attack were the people who entered the building. Every floor had at least one person spreading the poison.

Death occurs in one to ten minutes after inhalation.

The first person to die from it did so alone, on Level C of parking deck 6. She felt a tightening in her chest, and her nose began running. She tried to walk, but lost control of her muscles and fell to the concrete. Her limbs began twitching and her lungs lost the ability to pull in air. She died from asphyxia within two minutes of breathing in the gas.

Two people found her five minutes later. Both of them lived another five to six minutes. They had time to call for EMTs, who wouldn't arrive for another fifteen minutes.

The first person to make it through the FBI doors hadn't been touched by the gas until he was five feet from the entrance. A small amount landed gently on his right shoulder, sinking through the fabric and touching his skin. He was lucky not to breathe it in. He lasted another sixteen minutes.

During that time, he passed twenty-three people on the way to his desk, including the four he'd stood next to in the elevator. Three of those four felt their sinuses fill in a matter of seconds. One of them even commented on it, drawing strained laughter from everyone in the elevator.

Two died face down at their desk. The other fell at a urinal, his skull cracking on the porcelain. Blood trickled onto the floor as the urinal flushed, triggered by the movement of his collapse.

The final death toll was 83%. The intervention of emergency personnel pushed that number down, giving their lives to honor their training. The highest rate of death was among the children affected.

Throughout the building, people lay shivering and shaking on the carpeted floors. They drooled, urinated, and defecated on themselves as they lost control over their bodily functions. They suffocated in large spasms, their bodies jerking as if an invisible force moved them at will.

By the time medical professionals arrived with the correct equipment to help, there wasn't much they could do, other than quarantine the area.

The hundred and fifty cars that had been outfitted with the gas ended up affecting over nine hundred employees, sixty-three emergency personnel, one hundred and fifty-nine contractors, and forty-three children.

Even Director Alan Waverly was affected. The poison was not limited by badges or secret elevators that only he could access. The alarm system went off five minutes before he was infected, but at that point, no one knew what was happening. Some medical professionals suspected, but no sarin experts had yet arrived and the etiology of the attack had not yet been identified.

Waverly's chest tightened, just as those of the employees below him had. His nose ran. He felt his arms begin twitching, and then he collapsed on the floor. His assistant rushed to help him, infecting herself as well. Before long, she was lying next to her boss, both of their bodies doing the jitterbug.

The plane flew over the Midwest desert, its occupants heading for the east coast.

"Will you turn it off, please?" Tommy whispered.

Veronica hit the button on the remote and killed the television. The sarin attack had been on the news and Tommy didn't want to watch any more of it. Everything he needed was feeding into the computer on his lap, and listening to the talking heads go on and on about the attack did nothing for him.

"What happened to him last night?" Tommy whispered.

Christian sat across from Tommy, as he had on the first plane ride across the desert. His eyes were closed. He had retreated into his mansion without offering any reason or motive. Even the plane taking off hadn't jolted him from wherever he had gone.

"Nothing. We talked a bit before bed, then I fell asleep."

"You didn't hear any of his conversation with Luke?"

Veronica shook her head.

No one had slept since Christian woke them, alerting them to Luke's latest threat. They had been preparing all morning, and in the end, no one had a chance. The death toll was rising by the minute, those that the sarin had poisoned but not killed dying in the hospital.

"Then what is this about?" Tommy said, glancing at Christian before returning his gaze to Veronica.

"How do I know, Tommy? I've seen what you've seen. Nothing else."

Tommy stared at her, his gaze that of an experienced detective who knew he was being bullshitted.

"When we came out here," he said, "your attitude had changed. I saw you thirty minutes before we left, and you were happy. By the time we boarded the plane, you were different. What happened in those thirty minutes, Veronica? Don't lie to me again. You asked me to share with you, and I did. Now it's your turn. This is important."

Veronica looked down at her computer. Tears were in her eyes, but Tommy couldn't wipe them away. He wouldn't have, even if he could. He would have let her cry until she spilled her guts if that's what it took to get to the truth.

"Veronica. What happened before the plane ride?"

She closed her eyes and a tear fell out. "He said I could tell you when the time was right, but it isn't, Tommy. He isn't going to do it."

"Do what?"

She opened her eyes and Tommy saw fire in them. "Why? Why are you making me betray his trust?"

"Look at him. Do you think he's okay right now? Whatever he told you, he's keeping it from Waverly. More importantly, he's keeping it from *me*. No one, goddamn *no one*, has lost as much as I have. So for him to keep it from me is fucking nonsense. For you to keep it from me is nonsense. Whatever he's hiding, it has material bearing on this case, doesn't it?"

She said nothing.

"Doesn't it?" Tommy asked with as much force as he could.

Veronica nodded.

"Exactly. Now tell me what he said."

She hesitated for a few more seconds, but Tommy saw her walls crumbling. Whether it was from their conversation about black clouds and suicide, or his current plea, he didn't know and didn't care.

"Luke told him that if he killed us—you, me, and Waverly—that he would turn himself in. That all of this would stop if he killed us three."

"Jesus Christ," Tommy whispered, closing his own eyes. That's why Christian had gone into his mansion. Why he hadn't said a word since everything happened this morning. Because he thought he could have stopped it, and all he needed to do was murder his friends.

Veronica nodded miserably.

"Jesus Christ," Tommy said again, the full weight of the burden Christian had been carrying hitting him.

"What are you going to do?"

Tommy was quiet for a long time. "I don't know yet."

Christian watches Luke when Luke was a boy.

A week has passed since the cathedral burned nearly to the ground. The fire department arrived late, and their equipment wasn't modern enough to put out the blaze.

The preacher man was admitted to the hospital with his lungs full of smoke.

Now a week later, he is standing on the cracked stoop of Luke's house.

Luke is walking down the street. His book bag is on his back, and his brother is walking beside him on his left.

"Stop," he says when he sees the preacher man. He's pale and sickly looking, but he's there all the same. As are the two men he brought with him.

His brother listens to him, knowing that when Luke speaks, he's never wrong. If Luke wants him to stop, then he best do it.

"Listen to me," Luke says, his eyes not leaving the preacher man. He doesn't look at his brother as he speaks. "I want you to go back to school. Go and tell whoever is there that you need to study some more. I'll come get you, but don't come back home until I'm with you, okay?"

"Okay, Luke. What's wrong? Why is Father Marquez at our house?"

"Just go, Mark," Luke says. "I'll come get you soon."

His brother turns and leaves. Luke waits for a few minutes, letting Mark get farther away. Whatever is about to happen, he doesn't want his younger brother to see it. The preacher man doesn't drop his gaze. He seems to understand what Luke is doing and is okay with it.

The priest nods. Luke doesn't turn away. He knows what the preacher man is saying.

It's time.

And, so it is. Luke continues along the street and turns right at the dirt driveway that contains no car.

"The wayward son," the preacher man says as Luke approaches the stoop. "Returned home."

The two men step out from behind Marquez. They're large and angry looking. They move to Luke without pausing. Each grabs an arm, although he is not resisting. They drag him up the steps. They simply want to be rough. The preacher man steps to the side, and they drag him into the house.

Christian watches Luke's face when he sees his mother on the couch.

She's hog-tied, her arms and legs fastened together. Blood is smeared across her frightened face.

Luke's eyes widen, but he quickly gains control of himself. He knows surprise is what they want to see. Anger. Hatred. Fear. Pleading. Emotions that he will not give them, because Luke knows it won't save his mother's life. Even at this young age, he knows people do not walk away from situations like this. Luke is certain his mother's life is over, and most likely his, too.

"Sit him down," the priest says.

The strong men do as they're told.

Marquez moves between Luke and his mother, cutting off the boy's line of sight to his mother.

"You burned my church down, son," the preacher man says as one of the thugs grabs a chair from across the room and places it behind Marquez. "Did you think there would be no consequences? Did you think you could do that and I would simply...what?" The preacher man looks around as if searching for an answer. "Just go away?"

He sighs and looks at Luke. "No, son. No, no, no. Do you know how many years I've been in this town, collecting payments for people's souls? Forty-two years. I'm sixty-four years old. One does not make it to this age by allowing any newcomer to shove them around." He paused and looked at the strong man behind Luke, a smile on the priest's face. "Though, I must admit, no one has tried doing it exactly as you have, nor for such foolish reasons. You burned down my church over what? A few thousand pesos each year?"

The priest spits on the floor. "A few thousand pesos. I piss that each morning." Marquez scoots his chair back, letting Luke see his mother. "Look at her. Look at what you've done. This is only the beginning, my son. Much more is to come. You're going to watch. Then, you're going to help build my church back up, brick by brick, and then you're going to keep paying me, just as your mother did. Do you understand? You're going to make me whole, my son."

Luke hears the words, his agile mind filing them away for later, but he cannot pull his eyes from his mother. He does not show any emotion, but it's there below the surface. He looks at the priest. "Let her go and I'll do whatever you want."

"No. That time has passed. A time for sowing and a time for reaping, that is what the good Lord tells us. You have sowed, and now you will reap."

The priest stands and the thug's strong hands clamp down on Luke. He does not try to move, not until the other man yanks down his mother's pants, leaving her naked bottom in the air.

Now Luke struggles. He struggles and spits and swears, all his strength focusing on freeing his mother. The strong man slaps him to the floor. His large hand leaves both a red print and blood on the boy's face.

Forcing Luke to watch, the priest rapes his mother.

Luke tries to stop the desecration of his mother. He lunges for the priest, but the second thug kicks him in the ribs and he collapses to the floor again. He spits blood through his broken teeth as the tears come.

Luke doesn't stop. He continues trying to attack the priest, although there is no hope.

The preacher man grows winded and collapses on the

couch. One of his men steps forward and shoots Luke's mother in the face, spreading blood and bone across the floor.

Luke sees it all, and so does Christian.

The television shuts off, leaving Christian alone with the Other.

"He couldn't save her," Christian said.

"Nope. Sure couldn't," the Other agreed.

"Is it connected, this and that?" Christian didn't even realize he was talking to the Other, bouncing ideas off him like a sounding board.

"You tell me. You're the one that keeps coming back here, watching these ancient videos."

Christian stood from the chair and turned around to stare at Luke's floor.

"He's not going to stop unless I do what he wants. He'll keep killing. Why does he want me to kill those I love? Does he somehow feel guilty for what happened to his mother? Does he feel like he killed her?"

Luke said his purpose was to create discord, to actively affront God. Was that a decoy, or simply a lie he told himself? Did something else drive Luke to do these things? Was it guilt?

"You keep asking yourself what's the reasoning behind all this, but does it matter?" the Other asked. "Isn't the important question whether or not you're going to acquiesce to his demand?"

Christian shook his head, but he said nothing. Action

was secondary when it came to Luke. What mattered was the reasoning behind it. That was how Christian would stop him, through understanding him.

Christian walked through the lengthy maze, heading to the last time he had seen Luke. The last time before all of *this* had started. Venezuela. It was near the maze's end.

A hologram shot down from the ceiling, creating a life sized simulation of what had happened. Christian stepped into his outline, standing where he had been when he'd exited the van.

Luke was in front of him, his face flashing to the approaching man on his right and halting him dead in his tracks. Christian stepped out of his outline and walked across the digital landscape. He moved past the armed agents with their weapons pointing at Luke. He paid no mind to their shouted orders for Luke to get the fuck down.

He'd been terrified when it happened, but that was in the past. Nothing in this scene could hurt him. He reached Luke just as he started staring at the Christian from the past. From where he now stood, the two were looking at each other.

The scene stopped when Christian stopped directly in front of his ex-partner.

The hard brown eyes had seen more than most people could imagine. Eyes that had seen things that would break grown men, let alone children.

"What are you after, Luke? Why do I have to kill them to make you stop? Is *that* an affront to God?"

Luke stared at him, no words exiting his mouth. If the scene started playing again, Christian would hear the previous conversation play out. It held no sway here, though. The answers Christian needed wouldn't be found in Venezuela.

"I'm not going to kill them," he said.

He heard blood dripping and knew that the Other stood next to him. He looked to his left, and sure enough, his alter ego was there.

"I'm not," he repeated, looking back at Luke.

"Forty-three children died," the Other said. He knew the number because Christian knew it. "Are another forty-three worth your friends?"

Christian wanted to say *yes*, but no words came. Because... Were his friends worth it? What would *they* say if they knew for certain that people would continue dying if they continued living?

It's not your decision to make. It's not Luke's decision to make. It's not even their *decision to make. They don't get to kill themselves because a madman is loose, and you certainly don't get to kill them for the same reason.*

"Maybe that's true. Maybe it's not," the Other said.

CHAPTER NINETEEN

Charles Twaller waddled up to the nurse's station. He held a dozen roses in his right hand. His left was empty.

"Hi, ma'am. I'm looking for my mother's room. She came in last night with all the other victims of that horrible attack."

The nurse looked up from her computer. Her face was a picture of exhaustion. Bags hung from her eyes, and sharp lines created crow's feet at the corners. Her face was pale and her brown eyes spoke of endless hours. His question, without a doubt, was creating *more* exhaustion.

"Sir, that area is quarantined. No one is allowed in."

"You can't be serious," Charles said. "I just drove twelve hours from Atlanta."

"I'm sorry, sir, but you'll have to wait. There's a waiting room that way to your right."

Charles turned his head to follow her pointed finger down the hall to the room full of people at the end. "Do you have any idea when the quarantine will be over?"

"No, sir. Not at the moment." She went back to her computer, not acknowledging him anymore.

"Thanks for your help." Charles turned and waddled down the hallway. The conversation had served its purpose. The place was light on security. Charles imagined that most of the DC police were still tied up with the gift he'd given the FBI office. If anyone had noticed him enter, his little show with the nurse would give him a few minutes.

He wanted to lay eyes on Christian Windsor and Tommy Phillips. He knew this was dangerous, but he didn't care. He wanted to see them before he put his hands on them. They knew what he looked like, but Charles wasn't too terribly worried about it.

The men he'd put on them in Boston had reported that they were leaving. Charles hadn't known where they were flying at first, but he'd made some phone calls and learned that the FBI Director had been affected during the attack. So, he'd made a few more calls and become convinced that the two were heading to the Director's hospital room.

Charles' men were sitting in the waiting room the nurse had gestured at, and had been for the past eight hours. He knew Phillips and Windsor had a workstation set up and the two of them were running their division from the hospital.

Charles didn't care. He was here to teach them that they didn't get to drop by his mother's house without repercussions. That, and to teach Titan a few things as well.

He entered the waiting room, holding his flowers so that the petals faced the ceiling. The room was packed tightly. Charles immediately saw the eight men he'd sent over here. They were spread throughout the room, some sitting in chairs, some leaning against the walls. All eight glanced up as he entered. That was their training, although Charles saw recognition in their eyes.

All this had been planned out over phone calls made the past twenty-four hours.

Charles waddled over to one of the only open spaces on the wall and leaned into it. The people to his left and right adjusted their positions, making way for his short, fat body.

The invalid and the genius were here as his men had told him. They were sitting at a small makeshift table and staring at the genius' computer, neither noticed Charles' entrance.

These were the two men Titan wanted so desperately? They looked... Well, one was barely living and the other was a thin piece of nothing. All of Titan's intelligence, and he was willing to give up his life and all of his wealth for these two?

No matter. Charles had seen enough.

He looked at one of the men standing against the wall and nodded. The man wasted no time. His gaze moved from his boss' as he stepped out of the waiting room.

More men were waiting outside, and it was time to place them inside.

"I've got to pee," Christian said.

"Well, you don't need permission," Tommy responded.

He pushed his chair back from the small table and

glanced at Tommy. It had been a bit of trouble getting the table in here, but they had to keep working. They weren't physically out there looking, but reports were coming in constantly and there was no one else to monitor them.

They had spoken briefly about not waiting here. It might have been better to stay in the field. In the end, they'd decided against it. Tommy wasn't able to be in the field for long anymore, and Waverly had waited in the hospital with the two of them. They could do as much here, maybe more as they were able to cast a wider net.

Christian pushed his chair underneath the table. "You need me to empty you?" he asked, indicating the catheter's bag.

Tommy shook his head. "No, we just did it an hour or so ago. Should be good."

Christian nodded and headed for the hallway with his eyes on his feet. He stopped as he exited the room. Something was bothering him, although he wasn't sure what it was.

He hated when his mind shot up a flare when he was too exhausted to focus. Christian trusted the flares. He hadn't back when they'd been warning him about Luke, but now he never doubted them. His mind wanted him to know *something*.

Christian closed his eyes tightly, forcing the rest of the world away. He'd seen something in the room, but it was hidden from him. He'd been too concerned with leaving and had missed whatever was there. He started to turn around—

No. Keep moving. Down the hallway. Quickly.

Christian opened his eyes and did as his mind told him.

He trusted it implicitly. It was the only thing in this world that he could count on regardless of what else happened. He rounded the corner and found himself in front of the restroom door.

He paused, hoping that his mind was ready to push something up to the top. Nothing.

Christian opened the bathroom door and walked inside. The door closed behind him…and then the lights went off.

He would never have Luke's reaction time. He would never be able to fend off an attacker as Luke had him back in the hotel room. Yet, for once, his mind and body were in unison.

Christian heard someone moving on his left. He didn't think as he moved, his feet working perfectly. He backed up just in time to avoid something swinging through where his face had been.

Feeling the air rush past him, Christian fell backward purposefully. His ass hit the floor and he slid away from whoever was attacking. His right hand struggled briefly for the pistol on his hip. The lighted emergency exit sign on the wall outlined the man coming directly at him. He was wasting no time.

Christian freed his weapon, aimed at his assailant, and pulled the trigger. The resulting boom was deafening, his ears ringing from the echo of the discharge in the enclosed area.

The man stopped in his tracks and Christian fired again without thinking. There was no time to think. If there were consequences for this, he'd have to deal with them later.

The man collapsed to the floor. Christian didn't move. He couldn't hear anything besides the ringing in his ears. He breathed in and out in large gulps, but kept his weapon pointed at the man.

After a few seconds, he stood and shuffled to the door. His hands were shaking so badly that he barely kept hold of his weapon. He pulled on the door handle, expecting light to flood the restroom, but the hallway was just as dark.

He heard what he hadn't been able to inside. The sound of screams and gunfire blazing down the hallway.

A woman turned the corner, illuminated by another emergency exit sign. She was screaming, her mouth open in a wide O. A bullet caught the side of her head and ripped through her skull. She crashed into the opposite wall, her mouth still open. Blood that looked more like oil splashed against the wall as she slid down it.

Christian's chest heaved and tears welled in his eyes as his emotions threatened to overwhelm him. He fell back against the bathroom door and it opened beneath his weight. He slipped inside, letting it close in front of him.

Is this a panic attack? some piece of him asked.

Nothing was in control enough to answer. Sweat dripped from his face and he felt himself growing light-headed. His gun dropped to the ground and clattered into a corner. He couldn't tell whether his vision was darkening or it was only the blackness of the room.

Christian hit the ground on his knees, his hands smacking on the tiles.

A voice boomed over the hospital's intercom system. He didn't know if what he heard was real or in his mind.

"Christian Windsor, you're needed in the waiting room." A shrill giggle came next, sounding like both a small girl and a grown man. A few seconds passed as the giggler got his laughter under control. "Seriously, Christian. Come to the waiting room. We don't have much time."

"It won't end," Christian said. "None of this will end."

It wouldn't, and he knew it with such certainty that God himself might as well have spoken. Luke would not stop. Whoever was giggling over the intercom was one of his minions, another heinous creature he'd put on Christian's path.

Luke would never quit. All the pain and terror he created would continue forever. It didn't matter if Christian left the restroom and went where the man on the intercom commanded. It didn't matter if he hid here and waited it out. Luke would still come.

He was an unstoppable force. He would always be there, and what could Christian do?

He glanced at the corner where the gun had fallen.

"You could kill yourself," the Other said. The emergency exit's red glow shone down on the long, black rivers running from his dripping eyes and falling to the floor in a dark rain. "That would end it all. That would make sure nothing else he ever does will matter in the slightest. Let him have his party. But why don't you check out from it?"

Christian stared at the negative version of himself with blurry eyes.

It sounded so good. So easy. So...

"Painless. Because once you do it, there will be no more pain. None."

"Tommy," his mother said from behind him. "Tommy is still out there and —"

"*Chrriiissttiiiaannn,*" the voice sang over the intercom.

His mother waited until the voice finished. "Tommy is out there, Christian. He could have killed himself at any time, but he kept going. It might be hate that drives him, but he's still in the car. So don't you dare get out now. You joined the FBI to help people and make a difference. So *do* it. You get *up* and defend those innocent people. Get up and go get your friend."

"Pain waits out there," the Other said. "In here, you can find peace."

"Go get your friend," his mother countered.

Christian closed his eyes. The tile felt cold beneath his fingertips and knew the gun's metal would feel similar.

There wasn't time to go into his mansion, but in his moment of pain, Christian remembered Luke.

Months pass and Luke does nothing. He and his brother move into the local orphanage that is supported by the Catholic Church. Father Marquez sits on the orphanage's board.

The brothers remain silent and go to work every day helping rebuild the cathedral. Luke says nothing about what happened, and Mark doesn't ask about it.

Luke learns the construction trade over those three months. He dreams of his mother each night during this period. His brother slips deeper and deeper into a depression that Luke cannot pull him from.

Those three months are some of the darkest of Luke's life. There will be times in the future that are just as hard, but by then he will be more capable of handling them. Luke considers suicide. It's an odd thought for him, one that carries very little emotion with it.

He simply thinks, *Maybe this isn't worth it.*

Maybe he's right.

However, there is his brother to consider. What would Mark do without Luke? Especially with Marquez in charge of the orphanage. Then there is Marquez himself. Luke sees him from time to time. The priest never looks at him or speaks to him. The preacher man goes on about his business as if he had no part in the destruction of Luke's family.

Luke refrains from committing suicide, but only out of a strange fascination. He begins to think that killing the priest should occur *first*. Then, once that is accomplished, he will be free to go.

It's three in the morning when Luke arrives at the preacher man's new house. It's a simple structure a couple of miles from the church. Luke knows he could have afforded any home he wanted. This one is for appearances. The preacher man will live here until his cathedral is finished, and then he'll move back inside the church.

Luke walks from the orphanage to Marquez's temporary house. The walk takes a little over an hour and he has a light sheen of sweat across his forehead by the time he arrives. He doesn't pause or try to hide when he reaches the lawn. He walks across the grass at the same pace he walked here. His head is raised, and while he knows someone might be watching him, he doesn't care.

The priest must die, and then Luke can die as well.

He reaches the small porch and pulls on the screen door. It opens with a squeak. The sound doesn't bother Luke. He is *un*botherable.

He tries twisting the doorknob but it doesn't turn. The preacher man doesn't feel safe enough to leave his door open, not even in a neighborhood that loves him so. Perhaps he isn't as beloved as he's led people to believe, and perhaps he knows it.

The locked door is simply another obstacle in Luke's path. He does not personalize it any more than he would a strong wind blowing down the road. He moves to the right of the porch and hops off it. There is a window on the side of the house. He briefly looks at the window and realizes that it's also locked.

Luke scans the ground around him and sees a few rocks lying in the grass. He finds one that fits nicely in his hand, then turns back to the window. It is low to the ground, so he doesn't need to pull himself up to it. He takes a few steps back, and then throws the rock.

The window breaks with a crash that echoes through the night.

Luke steps up to the shattered window and knocks out the stray pieces, creating an opening he can maneuver through without getting cut.

"*Who's there?*" the preacher man shouts from inside.

Luke says nothing as he climbs through the window. He's inside the house now and still feels calm, as if all of this was preordained.

As if God wanted him here to stop this false prophet.

"*Who's out there? I'm a priest! I'm this town's priest!*"

Luke hears the man's panicked voice and walks across the house to it.

"I know," he says as he enters the preacher man's bedroom.

A small light burns on the nightstand, casting Marquez in a yellow glow. Even so, he looks pallid, like a waxy ghost.

"You," he says. The word isn't laced with hate, but made from it. "You… *Get out!*"

Luke only shakes his head and pulls a small pocketknife from his pants.

"Hey! Hey! *No!*" Marquez shouts.

Luke walks toward the bed and the priest scoots backward, pushing himself against the wall behind him.

"What are you doing, son? What the hell do you think you're doing?"

Luke stares at him for a second. Another moment is here. One that will shape the young man's life, shaping him into a man, and then perhaps an old man. Luke has had a lot of these moments in a short time.

He doesn't understand that yet. He only knows that he is going to kill someone.

The speed with which he slashes reveals the underlying athleticism that will assist so often as he grows older. He slices the priest's face open, splitting his skin like an over-ripe avocado.

The meat inside spills out across his pale skin and he screams. The preacher man screams a *lot*.

Luke hears him, but only as a wolf hears a rabbit's squeal, or perhaps as a clockmaker hears the internal mechanisms of a piece he is working on.

He moves the knife across the priest's chest. The blade isn't long, but Luke works almost preternaturally. He cuts the priest perfectly from his right nipple down to just below the left of his ribcage. From there, Luke drags the blade across his stomach to the right side, and the priest's intestines spill out onto his legs.

The priest is not screaming now. He is in shock, staring down at his guts burning hot on his legs as if he can't understand why they are no longer inside as they're supposed to be.

Luke takes a step back, the red life leaching from the preacher staining his hands. He ignores the man's guts, staring at his face instead.

Marquez is growing paler as the blood exits his body in pulsing rivers. His heart is still pumping, trying to do its job, but it's growing weaker by the second. Luke doesn't pull away or shy from his act. He stares at the priest the way the criminals he will one day chase stare at their victims. Taking it all in.

The priest gives out a death rattle, as if an actual rattlesnake rests in his throat, and then he is no more. Only his body is left, a disgusting slab of meat.

Luke stares a second longer before leaving the house. He goes to the orphanage and gets his brother. Then, at the age of eleven, he and his brother leave Mexico.

Luke has decided not to kill himself. Partly because of his brother, but that is not everything.

Not by a long way.

Christian opened his eyes, only seconds having passed since he closed them.

"Mr. Windsor, please report to the principal's office!" A squeal of laughter screeched from the overhead intercom.

Christian didn't see his mom or the Other. Only the dead body remained in the room with him. His eyes flicked to the gun in the corner, and he quickly moved to pick it up. There was blood on the grip. He wiped it away with his shirt.

It won't end.

He knew that now.

Luke wouldn't stop coming for him. He didn't even know the meaning of the word concede. He hadn't stopped when his mother was raped, and he certainly wasn't going to do so now. The man might have been more machine than human.

Christian raised his weapon.

He would continue as well, then. He would go get his friend. He'd keep putting one foot in front of the other until they stopped working.

He pulled the restroom door open and stepped out into the hallway.

Charles was having fun on the intercom system. More than he had thought possible, for sure. The invalid was next to him in the security station. There were televisions stacked against the wall, each showing high viewpoints from around the hospital wing. Charles focused on the TV that showed the waiting room.

He had six men waiting for Christian Windsor.

The invalid was quiet. Charles had thought about knocking him out, but decided what would be the point? It's not like he could get up from his chair and *do* anything.

"There he is!" Charles shouted, his eyes catching sight of Windsor on a different screen. He was stepping out of a restroom, his gun raised. "Oh, this is *good*."

Charles glanced at the invalid, wanting to see his facial expression. But the creep wore no expression. Fucking invalid couldn't react, and where was the fun in that? "I don't know why you want to continue living. I would have ended it the first chance I got."

The invalid didn't so much as glance at Charles. He kept his eyes focused on the screens.

Charles scoffed. He might not have much in the way of facial expressions, but at least he was interested. He watched as Windsor moved down the hallway. From the vantage point inside the security station he could see the hall's cross section as well.

He picked up his two-way radio. "I've got eyes on him. He's three hallways up and to the right. One of you go get him."

Windsor crept slowly along the corridor, looking everywhere as he walked. Charles didn't think he was trying to be careful. He was scared. Terrified, even. "Your friend isn't the bravest, is he?"

Without moving anything but his mouth, the invalid whispered, "He's coming, isn't he?"

"Hah!"

The invalid was right. Windsor was heading toward the waiting room, which was exactly where Charles wanted him. Time was short and Charles knew it. SWAT would arrive within the next twenty minutes.

He'd taken some precautions. Even so, he couldn't hide here forever. The sound of gunfire had probably already been heard elsewhere in the hospital, although not by anyone working *here*. His men had systematically moved through the wing and killed any security guard, nurse, or visitor they'd seen. They'd left the patients alone, but not out of mercy. No one wanted to be around possible sarin contamination.

Two of the men from the waiting room were moving down the hall now, their weapons raised. They would reach Windsor in the next few seconds.

He had stopped at the corner, his back to the wall and his gun held by his face. His eyes were closed.

"What's he doing? Praying?" Charles asked, expecting no answer. He hoped his men didn't kill the bastard. Their pay would drop stupendously if *that* happened. He wanted his fun first.

"He's counting," the invalid said.

"What the fuck do you mean, he's counting?"

"Your men's footsteps."

Charles mouth opened to say something else, but no words left his mouth.

Onscreen, Christian-fucking-Windsor dropped to one knee and pivoted into the hallway. He fired two shots and Charles heard their echoes.

His men dropped to the floor, their bodies falling like bags of flour.

Windsor waited on his knees for a second, the gun

pointing at the men as if the dead might still rise. When they didn't, he stood again.

Charles grabbed the two-way. "He's coming. Go get him. *Do not fucking kill him.*"

The remaining four men emptied out of the waiting room.

Christian's breath felt heavy, his lungs burning deeply. He wasn't on the verge of hyperventilating, but he was on the verge of *being* on the verge. He walked by the two men he'd dropped moments before, not looking down at the holes his shots had punched into them.

They'd been sloppy on their approach, which meant that they underestimated him. He couldn't have killed them if he hadn't heard their footfalls. He had known precisely where they would be when he'd fired on them and his shots had been true.

However, they would not be the last of them, and Christian knew it.

Another bullet tore through the hallway, tagging high and hitting the ceiling above his head. Christian flashed into a hallway on his right. He couldn't see where the bullet had come from. The hall was too dark even with the light from the emergency signs.

"*Windsor!*" the man in charge screamed from the intercom. "*If you don't give up, you're dead! There's too many for you to escape from!*"

Christian stood with his back to the wall.

"*Put the gun down and you'll make it out of here alive!*"

Waverly, he thought. *Is he hearing this? Can everyone in the hospital hear what is happening, or is it just this wing? Is anyone coming?*

He couldn't answer the question, and more bullets hit the wall opposite him. They were pinning him down, trying to scare him into dropping his weapon.

"There's no way out, bucko," the man on intercom said, erupting into more squealing laughter. "Drop it!"

"Where's Tommy?" Christian shouted.

A pause came from both the weapons and the intercom.

"One more time. What was that?"

"Where's Tommy?"

"Put the gun down and you can come see him," the intercom said.

"Is he alive?"

Another brief pause, Christian imagining that whatever he said was being relayed back to the man behind the intercom.

"He is, of course! I've got fun things planned for the three of us. Lots of them!"

Christian knew he couldn't gun this many men down. Hell, he couldn't even see them all.

Go get your friend, his mother had said.

Fighting right now wouldn't accomplish that. Going forward with his weapon drawn would be suicide. If he'd wanted that, he didn't have to walk here in the first place.

Christian knelt and threw his gun into the hallway.

"Good! Boys, take him!" the man on the intercom said.

And take him, they did.

CHAPTER TWENTY

"Dr. Titan, how are you doing today?"

Charles knew Titan was aware of what had happened the previous night. He only needed to turn on a television to see that the world was burning. Every station was transfixed by the horrors being inflicted upon this great nation, and there were a lot of them at the moment.

"I'm well," Titan said.

Despite being in complete control, Titan's strange calm raised goosebumps across Charles' arms. "You've seen the news?"

"I have. You've been busy, and not in the way that we agreed."

"That's true. I have been busy. I'm a busybody, you might say. Fuck our agreement, Luke. Do you mind if I call you Luke, Luke? I'm sure you don't, given how much money has changed hands between us. Well, Luke, fuck our agreement. The new agreement is this. I'm going to kill your wonder boy and his partner, and if you decide to show up, I'll kill you too. How's that sound?"

"Is he still alive, my wonder boy?" Titan asked.

"For now, yes. That's going to change, soon enough."

"Where are you, Mr. Twaller?"

"No, no. I don't think we'll go into that right now. You're a smart guy, right, Luke? You can figure out that problem in no time at all."

"Perhaps. Are you with him now?"

Charles was feeling more off balance by the second. In a single night, he had halted Titan's entire operation and stolen the person he wanted most, yet this man sounded like they were discussing a play they might see later.

"He's around," Charles said.

"I want you to ask Christian what happened with my brother. Will you do that for me, Mr. Twaller?"

"Why don't you tell me?"

"Christian will probably know the story better than I do. It was a long time ago for me, but I imagine he thinks of it often. Ask him. I'll see you soon, Mr. Twaller."

Titan ended the call. Charles sat with the phone still pressed to his ear, barely believing what he'd just heard.

He would see *Charles* soon? As if he had planned all this out?

Charles shook his head, the sway of his flabby jowls making him look like a cow having a seizure.

"No. No. *No*! I'll see you soon, you stupid fuck!"

It took him a few minutes to calm down. Charles had transported the invalid and Windsor up north. He walked across the warehouse they were at on the edge of Baltimore, in one of the rundown factory districts. Charles had a lease for the warehouse, although he didn't use it, not even to store weapons when they came through.

The invalid lay face up on a mattress. Charles thought about letting him stew in his own filth as he pissed and shit himself, but decided against it. He didn't want to have to deal with the stench when he came in here to handle business, so he'd assigned a guard to those necessities.

Charles was making Windsor stand. Sturdy chains hooked through the cuffs on his wrists, holding him to the metal fence. He could swing slightly on the chains, but he couldn't bring his arms down completely. He was forced to either stand or hang from them.

Windsor's face was so bruised, he looked like an over-ripe peach that had been handled roughly. His right eye was swollen shut and his lips were nearly as big as sausages. The guys had beaten him mercilessly when they got to him.

Which was fine with Charles. He didn't mind in the slightest.

"I spoke to your ex-partner," Charles said as he approached the fence.

Windsor could still see out of his left eye. His chains rattled as he turned his face to focus on Charles.

"He wanted me to ask you something. He said you should tell me about what happened to his brother. What's that mean?"

"It means you're going to die wishing for that moment to come sooner," Windsor said, his words slurring thickly over his swollen tongue.

Charles scoffed. "Is that your autism coming out? Are

you unable to keep from saying whatever the hell you're thinking?"

Windsor shrugged. "It's truth."

"So, Titan is going to kill me to save you?" Charles asked.

Windsor spat blood. "I don't know what he wants with me. You're going to die. That's what the story about his brother means."

Charles smiled and gestured to the men around them. "We're pretty well guarded here. I think we'll survive. He's going to show up? You think that's what he was telling me."

"No, you fat fuck," Windsor said. "You're going to *die*. That's what he was telling you. I don't know if he'll show up. I don't know if he'll bomb the entire place with nuclear weapons. No one knows what Luke will do. If he wants you to hear about his brother, then that's the only thing you can take as gospel. You'll die screaming."

Charles felt a momentary rise of anger at the derogatory remark, but he pushed it away. He would indulge in rectifying the offense later. Well, sooner rather than later. Now wasn't the time. Windsor would pay for calling him a fat fuck, but he needn't pay just yet.

"Tell me about Titan's brother," Charles said.

Windsor's swollen right eye stared blindly at Charles. "It doesn't matter. That's not the point. If he told you to ask me, the message was simple. What happened to his brother is irrelevant to that message."

Charles' thick hand flashed up and slapped Windsor across the face. "I'll tell you what matters and what doesn't. You tell *me* what the fuck happened to his brother."

Windsor let out a dark laugh. "Luke was the elder. He was seventeen, and I think his brother was fifteen…"

CHAPTER TWENTY-ONE

Mark is indeed fifteen years old, and Luke is seventeen. Six years have passed since Father Marquez met his end and the two of them live in the United States.

Luke's last name is not yet Titan, but the time is growing close to when he will change it, forever concealing his past under a dark shadow.

Mark and Luke are in high school. Luke is thinking about applying for colleges. They live alone in a small apartment in Dallas, Texas. Luke handled the paperwork to ensure that continues. He didn't want to move far when they left Mexico, but he needed to get to a place where their American heritage wouldn't be a burden.

His days are simple, if hard. He wakes up at six. He and Mark arrive at school an hour later. From there, Luke moves through the school day without much trouble. His mind laps his teachers, although he is careful to keep that from being noticed. He remembers what happened when he was younger and made a fool out of a teacher. He does not have that luxury anymore.

Now, he lives his life for his brother, doing everything in his power to make sure their simple life is a good one. He leaves school at two in the afternoon. Mark does not come with him since he still has another hour of classes, and another hour of study hall after that. He isn't slow by any means, but Luke insists he stay for all the after school programs that will assist with his grades.

Luke heads to work. He flips chicken at a fast food restaurant every weekday from 2:30 until close at 10:00PM. After his shift, he catches a bus back home, usually bringing his brother something to eat. He doesn't like feeding Mark fast food so often, but even with his job, money is *always* tight.

Luke thinks the hard parts of his life are over. What happened in Mexico didn't happen to a *different* person. He remembers everything, and no matter how much he may want to, he can't wish the memories away.

However, he is moving beyond it. He focuses on his brother and the small life they have in America. That helps. He still has nightmares about his mother, and he isn't sure whether those will ever disappear.

The tough part is over, though. Or, at least, that's what he thinks. He tells himself nothing that happens in the future will ever be as bad as what happened in the past.

He tells himself that, but part of him doesn't believe it. Later in life, Luke will understand that he controls his destiny. At seventeen, he doesn't believe that yet. A part of him says that life, the universe, or more probably, God, isn't done with him yet.

He feels this most strongly when he wakes up from the nightmares about his mother.

He wakes up covered in cold sweat, with the mental image of that old priest having his way with her burned into his mind. Tears are in his eyes and he's breathing heavily, though he quickly gets it under control so as not to wake Mark.

It's then, in the early morning hours, that fear washes over him. Something is going to happen. Another one of those moments that he can't control, but will only be able to make a decision about.

That time is nearly here, the moment has almost arrived.

The church killed Luke's mother, but it is God who kills his brother.

Moments define Luke, as they do us all. What came next was the final one that defined him. The moment that turned a troubled but good kid into someone the *world* would come to fear.

Luke doesn't see any of the signs because he's working too much. He won't carry that weight forever. In the end, Luke sheds guilt and responsibility like a serpent does its skin.

There *are* signs, though, and Luke sees them when he thinks about it later.

His brother's appetite should have been the first clue. The change is subtle, and that's part of the problem. Had it been severe, Luke would have noticed regardless of how many hours he was working.

It wasn't.

It starts with Mark not asking for an extra chicken sandwich at dinner.

Then, he's not finishing his own sandwich.

Luke is tired. Exhausted really. Much later, he will be able to go for days without sleep while still functioning at extremely high levels. Now, he's seventeen and his body is still growing. He forces himself to power through each day, but a constant cloud of exhaustion rests over him, ready to drench him if he allows it.

Luke doesn't notice what is happening until he finds his brother passed out next to the toilet.

There's blood. A lot of it. It covers the inside of the toilet bowl and leaks from his brother's mouth onto the white tile. It's bright red and Luke is frightened. Panic threatens to settle in. This is his brother, his last connection to this world.

His only connection.

Luke doesn't shove the panic away. That might not have been possible even if he tried. He doesn't give in to it, though. He would have been lost in it.

Instead, he ducks it, maneuvering away like a boxer shirks an opponent that is getting too close. He drops to his knees beside his brother, smearing blood both on himself and across the floor.

He picks up his brother's head and places it in his lap, petting him and saying, "Mark, Mark, wake up, Mark. Wake up, buddy."

His voice is calm at first. Gentle. But he slowly picks up the urgency until he screams in the small bathroom.

"*Mark!*"

His brother doesn't respond.

Luke gets him to the hospital. He doesn't even think about calling emergency services. He steals a car from the street below his apartment—he taught himself how to hot-wire years ago. He hops the curb at the emergency room, then runs to the other side of the vehicle and pulls his brother out of the car.

He carries his fifteen year-old sibling in without realizing how easy it is for him. Those around him do. However, they chalk it up to adrenaline and not Luke's skeletal density and muscle mass.

Nurses ask Luke about his parents as they take his unconscious brother. They strap Mark to a gurney and are trying to pull Luke away, but he won't go. He stands right where he is and watches as they wheel his brother down the hallway.

"Where are you taking him?"

The same calmness that will frighten Charles Twaller so badly later in life is in his voice now. It's as if his emotions have died and left a shell behind. One that understands the crucial business at hand and will handle it regardless of the cost, but will do so without emotional investment. He has none to give.

The nurse has seen shock before, but this is something else. "They're taking him to run tests and make sure he's comfortable," she tells him in the voice professionals use to talk to stubborn children and madmen. "He's going to be fine, and you'll be able to see him soon. I need to ask you some questions. If you'll come with me over here, I would really appreciate it."

Luke stands his ground for another second, watching them wheel his brother away. Then he decides to go with the woman. The nurse leads him to a small check-in desk. She goes to the other side and sits down before pulling up something on her computer.

He observes the entire endeavor, his mind memorizing the intricacies of everything going on around him.

Moments.

Some part of his mind knows what is happening to his brother. It is already beginning to prepare him for the inevitable. It is beginning to change, hardening into the force that the world will find hard to reckon with. Detaching him from everything else through observation and categorization.

The nurse asks him questions about his parents and Luke doesn't respond at first. He knows it will create problems. He also knows it has nothing to do with helping his brother.

"I will tell you about my parents when you tell me what is happening with Mark."

The nurse looks at him with shock. She quickly gets herself under control, but she sees something different in the young man. There is someone barely older than a child standing in front of her, but that isn't what it feels like. She thinks, for a second, that she's looking at something time-less, and that freezes her to her core.

She tells Luke she'll be right back, but she doesn't return. She goes to a colleague and says, "You'll have to get him checked in. I'm not doing it." She means it. Wild horses couldn't have dragged her back.

Luke ends up giving them some information, but not everything they want. It creates more questions that will be answered later, but that doesn't bother him now. He just wants to be with his brother.

Four hours later, he's allowed to see him.

Mark is unconscious and a doctor is standing at the foot of his bed. Luke is to the right, looking down at his sleeping kid brother. His skin is pale, but there isn't any blood on his lips or smeared across his cheeks, and that is good.

"He has cancer," the doctor says. "It is a rare form. I won't say we've caught it *too* late, but it is in the latter stages."

Luke doesn't look away from the bed. "How late?"

The doctor hesitates before answering, "Stage four."

"There is no stage five," Luke says.

"No, there isn't."

Luke turns to look at the doctor. "Is my brother going to die?"

"I can't say for certain. No one can. There are options, although not many."

"Best case scenario?" Luke asks without tears in his eyes.

"He beats it."

"Worst case?"

"He dies within the month," the doctor says.

———

Luke and his brother fight. They fight hard. Mark begins chemotherapy and Luke forgets about school and work. The hospital figures out that they have no parents, though

Luke and Mark escape them finding records of what happened in Mexico.

Luke invents lies that take care of the details, but he isn't concerned with any of it.

His life consists of helping his brother live.

Luke prays. He prays almost constantly, even when he's feeding his brother or helping him walk to the bathroom as his strength fades. He prays, and he asks God for grace, for mercy, for anything that might give his brother life.

God doesn't answer, not in words and not in action.

His brother's cancer continues growing and spreading, the chemo doing virtually nothing to slow it down.

The doctor sits with Luke and tells him the truth, cold and harsh. "There's nothing else we can do."

"What do you mean?" Luke asks in that same oddly detached tone. He may be eating himself alive inside, but to the world, he's a machine.

The doctor finds it frightening, but says nothing. "We need to focus on making sure he's comfortable as he goes."

"No," Luke says. "There must be more we can do."

"There isn't, Luke," the doctor says. "You and your brother are two of the most courageous kids I've ever seen, but there is nothing we can do. There are options for how we can make sure the end comes without any pain for Mark. Do you feel like discussing them now, or do you need a bit of time?"

Luke discusses them but hears nothing.

His brain is on autopilot, answering questions while the core of his mind focuses on something else.

He goes to God. To that singular creature his mother

had taught him to believe was all loving, all knowing, all *everything.*

Even after the conversation with the doctor, Luke doesn't stop seeking God. His mind is rapidly running through calculations about the universe's size, speed, and expansion capabilities. He is trying to understand if there is a heaven and where it might exist. At the same time, he is praying harder than he's ever done before.

He finds himself in the hospital's chapel. It's the first time he's been in a church of any kind since he helped rebuild Marquez's. He kneels at the foot of the cross. There is no Jesus hanging on this one since the hospital is not Catholic.

He prays and prays with his eyes closed. He prays without any thought of quitting. He will continue this search for God until he finds an answer.

An hour passes, and another.

People move through the small chapel, but Luke doesn't look up or change position.

He prays, and finally, something happens.

Luke will go to his grave with the belief that God could not deny the force of will banging at his door and answered it. He will know that others would call what happened a hallucination. They will say he was under tremendous pressure and finally his mind snapped.

He will never care what other people might say. He knows the truth.

The room ceases to exist. *Luke* ceases to exist in any real sense of the word. There is only nothing, and that nothing stretches forever. It is a concept that cannot be understood unless it is experienced, but in the moment, Luke doesn't care.

He does not question where he is for a second.

He is in the mind of God.

He does not pause in awe or respect. He is raging. Luke is beyond the realm of right and wrong, beyond morality. He is in a place of such complete hate that the mind of God is simply a post that he will beat with his whip until his anger is abated.

"Make him live."

There is no answer.

"*Make him live*," Luke commands.

What happens is something that Luke will only share with one person, years and years from this moment. Christian Windsor. He will keep what he sees, hears, and feels to himself, but the moment defines him in a way that the others never could.

It changes not only the course of his life, but the course of history.

Words are spoken, but there is no voice that speaks them. They are simply *there*.

"Who is this that commands me?"

"*Make him live!*" Luke screams again.

"Simple child, leave me be."

All of Luke's rage and hatred pours out of him and into that nothingness. It spreads and fills and he somehow watches it approach God. This omniscient being is supposed to care. To love. To show mercy. Luke's words ring out across a space that doesn't exist.

"*You make him live!*"

"No."

Luke wakes up hours later.

He remembers everything, but says nothing to the preacher who finds him lying in front of the cross. Luke says nothing to anyone. He understands what he saw and he understands the meaning. His mother lied because someone lied to her.

Luke met God and knows that he cares nothing for his creations. God cares only for his own wants. He is a supremely selfish creature. Later, Luke will further refine his belief, but when he wakes up in the chapel, he simply knows that his brother will die and he can do nothing about it.

He spends some time with the doctor and decides it will be best if his brother dies at home, although that place is quickly changing too, now the authorities have learned there are no parents living with the two minors. They grant him space during his brother's final days.

Luke is by Mark's side when it happens. He holds his hand as his brother takes his last breath, gasping in short little heaves. Then, he's gone. His body is still there, but whatever made Mark, Mark, has departed. His body is thin and frail and looks like something that had never been alive at all.

An undertaker is called and Mark's body is removed.

Luke decides against a funeral. Mark's body is cremated and Luke does not keep the ashes. He saw the body in the bedroom and knew that there was nothing left of his brother, ashes or not.

The church took his mother, but Luke knew that God

had taken his brother. God, who holds the world in his hands, could not spare time nor a moment's peace for Luke. The being who Luke's mother believed was humanity's creator and savior had taken the last thing Luke had in this world.

God left Luke nothing, and so at seventeen, Luke decides he will take everything from God.

CHAPTER TWENTY-TWO

"And that means I'm going to die?" Charles asked.

Windsor nodded.

"What's his brother got to do with it?"

"I'd like to say I don't have time to sit here and explain this to you, but that's all I do have," the FBI agent said.

"Do I have to hit you in the face again?"

Christian smiled, though his fat lips hid most of his teeth. "I have a problem. I'm sorry."

"I wouldn't worry too much about it. You're gonna have more problems soon. A lot more. Now why does that story mean he's coming to kill me?"

"I never said *he's* coming."

"Then who is?"

"I don't know," Windsor said. "I only said Luke is going to kill you somehow."

Charles stared at his battered, blood crusted face. The blood painted dark wrinkles on it.

"Fine. Fucking fine. Why does that story make you think so?"

"His brother..." The FBI agent paused and looked up as if the answer would come from the ceiling above. "I didn't know this before, but when his brother died, that was the last time Luke was human. I don't mean that facetiously. There's something inside us..."

He looked down at Charles and seemed to consider his next words. Charles knew he was thinking of saying something along the lines of Charles not being human either, but the agent got control of his tongue before he caught another fist across the face.

"There's something inside us that separates us from animals. It separates Luke from us, too. Because he doesn't have it. It died with his brother. That ability to see another person and understand they're like you. To respect what's in them because you respect that it's in you, too. Luke lost that when his brother died. There is no one like him, in his mind. Maybe he's right. There is only him and this war he's created."

"What war? This one? The one we started?" Charles asked.

Windsor's one good eye met Charles' stare. "How much do you know about Luke?"

Charles shrugged. "I know what he hired me to do. That's it."

"What made you think it would be wise to halt what he hired you to do? To take me and my partner, and then try to kill Luke once he was angry?"

Charles said nothing. He wanted to slap the man again, but something in his voice kept Charles' hand at bay. Amazement. That was the emotion he heard. Windsor was truly amazed, but not at Charles' bravery or courage. He sounded amazed at his stupidity.

"I'll make this simple. Luke declared war on *God* after his brother died. Now, he's declared war on you."

———

Luke wondered if Mr. Twaller had asked Christian about his brother. He hoped so. He knew Christian's honesty would help Mr. Twaller understand what was coming, which was important. Luke wanted the man to anticipate his death. To worry about it.

Luke did not have time to dwell on his mistakes. Christian's—and to a lesser extent, Tommy's—life was in a very precarious position. His actions had to be perfect to ensure neither of them died. He could tolerate Tommy's death, but not Christian's.

Not yet.

Luke waited in a hotel room. He was sitting at a table with one leg crossed over the other and a glass of water in front of him. He had a pistol next to it. He wore black, leather gloves, but not to avoid any fingerprints. He planned on driving after this, and had purchased the car he wanted to make the drive in. A Tesla, of course.

The gloves were simply driving gloves. He wasn't worried about leaving prints for the FBI. They were in so much disarray that he wondered if they even knew Christian was missing. Mr. Twaller hadn't killed Waverly, but the Director's life wasn't guaranteed at the moment. The sarin attack was still working wonders, even after the fact.

The FBI had an interim director, and while Luke might

still be their major priority, finding him during this much chaos would be an exercise in futility.

The door to the hotel room opened. Luke was hidden from those entering, and would remain so until the door was shut. He picked up the gun and stood quietly.

The door closed and Luke fired the suppressed pistol.

The first person to enter dropped to the ground, leaving a mist of blood hanging in the air like a balloon of red paint had burst.

The second person to enter turned to the first as Luke put the gun down on the table. Her mouth hung open and abject terror spread across her entire face, but not a sound escaped her lips.

"Hi, Veronica," Luke said. "We have some work to do."

Keep reading for a sneak peek of the next book!

PREVIEW OF THE ANIMAL'S HUNT

Christian sees Luke a lot now. There is more light inside his head than out. He retreats to his mansion often. Especially when the pain grows too great to bear, as it has now.

Luke is eighteen and his brother is a year dead. His mother died seven years earlier. Luke was born with a different last name, but he is now Luke Titan.

After his brother's death, Luke spent time burying his history, the final piece being his name change. The boy who left a body, and a burned down cathedral behind him in Mexico no longer exists. Not legally, nor practically. Luke *Titan* is all remains of that person.

Christian watches him sit on a bench in front of a gorgeous building. A book is closed on Luke's lap. He hasn't opened it since taking a seat. It's the textbook for an introductory philosophy class that outlines Kant and Descartes, as well as a few other notable figures.

Luke does not need to read the book. He is well versed in all the philosophers. He goes to class because he knows it is expected of him and expectations are important.

He is an attractive young man. Thin and well dressed. He did not naturally have impeccable taste, but has spent much of his free time learning what clothes are in style and fit him well.

He notices the women passing him, or rather he notices when they glance at him. Many do. Even professors. He can read some of their thoughts, almost as if he is a telepath. He isn't, but their thoughts are written across their faces.

There is something stunning about Luke Titan sitting on a bench in the autumn sun. Christian can see it, too.

He's beautiful, Christian thinks. *Timeless.*

Luke watches the girl approach him. She is not beautiful in the same sense he is, but she's very pretty. Long blonde hair with dark blue eyes.

"You sit out here every day," she says as she arrives at his bench. "Why?"

"I have class in the building behind me." He smiles. It is both cocky and friendly.

"But why do you sit out here not talking to anyone?"

"I like the view," he says.

"Do you like it now?" she asks.

Luke's smile widens. "The view, at this moment, isn't bad at all."

"Then why don't you take this view on a date?" the girl asks. "I've watched you sit here for two weeks and you never once opened that book. So instead of sitting here, come get something to eat with me."

Luke's smile widens. "Are you asking me to ask you, or commanding me to take you out?"

"Both," the girl says.

"Well, would you like to get some food?"

"I thought you'd never ask."

The television turned off, leaving Christian sitting on Luke's floor inside his mansion.

"I haven't seen this one yet," the Other said.

He looked exactly the same as Christian except for the endlessly dripping blood seeping from his eyes, his hands, and sometimes even his mouth. The Other was something Luke left behind. One of *many* things, Christian supposed.

He could never tell, however, whether the Other was more Luke, or more himself.

"Neither have I," Christian answered.

He spoke to the Other now, and had been for the past few days—if days had actually passed. Christian didn't know. His usual grasp on time was failing between the pain and darkness that waited outside his mansion. He spoke to the Other because he thought he might go insane if he didn't.

"Did Luke write you any letters about this?"

"No," Christian said.

"So are you just making it up? Trying to entertain yourself so that you don't have to go back out there with the fat man?"

The fat man was Charles Twaller, and the question wasn't a bad one. Charles had captured both Christian and Tommy. Captured them, and was now in the process of slowly torturing them to death. That was where the pain outside originated from, and why Christian spent so much time inside his mental mansion, even if he only had this floor now.

"No, I don't think I'm making it up."

"Ha!" the Other shouted. "There's no way you know any of this for sure. You can't go downstairs anymore, and you don't want to be out in reality, so you're just making up stories to tell yourself."

Christian stood from the chair, ignoring the Other's taunting.

He walked across the top floor of the mansion. He didn't look at any of the sights on his left or right. He knew them all intimately. Every video and hologram was a piece of Christian's life that he spent with Luke Titan.

Right now, he wanted to see how far the water had risen.

He made his way to the floor's balcony and looked down the stretching staircase.

Christian was trapped up here by the flood rising from beneath. The water had filled half the stairwell, which meant the rest of his mansion was already flooded. Christian knew the water was a metaphor for his approaching death, his mind's best approximation for how much more torture he could take from Charles Twaller.

When the water reached this floor, Christian would drown. He doubted it would matter much by that point. He'd probably be close to brain dead by then.

"This Twaller man is pretty ruthless, huh?" the Other said, stepping up behind him.

"I love it when you state the obvious."

"Did you think Luke was going to save you?"

"I don't know. Maybe." Christian had considered it,

especially after Luke told Twaller to ask about his brother. "No, I didn't expect him to save *me*. I expected him to kill Twaller."

"You don't anymore?"

" I don't know," Christian said after a long pause. "If Luke was coming, he should have been here already."

"You don't even know how many days have passed. How can you say he should have already come?"

The Other was probably right. The torture was causing him to lose hope. The unending pain that would return the moment he left this place. Christian was capable of blocking it all out from his mansion, of somehow severing the brain/body connection. For a time, at least. He didn't know how it worked, was only grateful that it did.

"I have to go back," he said.

"Tommy?"

Christian nodded. *He* could come here and hide from the pain Twaller was inflicting. Tommy could go nowhere. Tommy was trapped in the small area they shared, lying on his cot as his body died.

"I've got to go," Christian said as if talking to a friend. The Other was no friend, though. He had no place in this mansion, no real place in Christian's life. Yet, right now, he was all Christian had.

"I'll be here when you get back," the Other said.

"I know you will. At least until the water reaches you."

"I'm as invested as you, Christian. I'd like Luke to save us all."

"Luke doesn't save," Christian said. "He just stretches his torture out over a longer timeline than Twaller."

Christian might have been giving up on rescue, but Charles Twaller was certain someone was coming. He didn't know if it would be Titan or the FBI, but *someone* would be here sooner or later.

The problem was that Charles had made up his mind to kill Titan as well as these two FBI agents, so he had to wait. However, the longer he stayed, the greater his chances of being apprehended.

Charles watched the two men he'd captured through closed circuit television, angry at his predicament. He had the lights on in their cell, although he kept them off most of the time. He only illuminated the area when he wanted to see them.

"This isn't good." Charles was alone in the Baltimore warehouse. There were other people here, but they were either on prisoner detail or preparing for when someone *did* show up.

"It's not goddamn *good*," Charles repeated. He knew he was talking to himself, but he didn't care. He certainly wasn't going to call his mother and talk to her. She was worrying, and what could he tell her? *Ma, remember those FBI jackasses who came by the house? Well, I've got them here and I'm looking at them right now. Lordy, I wish you could see this.*

No. That wouldn't help ease her worry much.

But Charles had to talk to someone, especially with how this was turning out. The invalid was near death, and the genius prick was getting close.

Phillips lay on the cot without moving. Charles had

stripped him naked and large burn marks marred his chest, arms, and legs. There was one on his nuts, too, although he'd only done that once. Charles didn't think it was too cruel, but putting the wires to Phillips's groin had caused his balls to swell after. He wasn't a doctor and didn't know if they might swell to the point of bursting, which in all likelihood would kill the invalid.

So, now he kept the electrical wires on other parts of his body.

It was funny, watching someone who couldn't move twitch like a paralyzed insect. Tommy jigged and jerked on the cot. He would fall onto the floor and keep on going until he either stretched the wires too far or Charles put an end to it.

When the shocks were over, he'd lie there unmoving again with smoke rising from his body. It was odd, watching someone whose body was dying be unable to feel the pain. The crippled man was being tortured to *death*, yet the real issue for him was mental. He knew his body was being destroyed and he was dying, but he couldn't *feel it*.

Still, there were some nice parts to watch. His mouth would clamp shut, spittle dripping from the corners of his lips, and a raspy noise escaping his throat. Charles giggled each time it happened. He couldn't help it.

The other one, Windsor, was receiving harsher treatment. His body was stronger.

He'd been stripped naked too, but Charles had been simpler in his methods of punishment. Large strips of flesh had been stripped from Windsor's chest and back with a whip. Both sides of his body were covered with bruises and swelling.

Charles had taken a few swings at the young man, but his giggles had overwhelmed him and he'd had to quit. It was how the whip removed the skin so quickly. He only had to bring it down on the prick's back, and the skin just disappeared as if the whip contained a magical cleaning formula.

He'd also had his men start flaying Windsor's arms. He was losing skin across large portions of his body. Charles enjoyed watching his men put the antibacterial salve on Windsor as well. It seemed to hurt him as badly as the actual torture. They used the salve to stave off infection, but Charles didn't know how long it would work.

He'd had them four days already, but they would die soon, and he knew it.

That's why this wasn't good. At all. He didn't want them dying before Titan arrived.

"Goddamnit," Charles said. "God-fucking-damn-it."

He stood, done watching them through the television. He waddled across the dilapidated warehouse and opened the door to the room holding his two prisoners.

The lights were still on overhead.

The invalid didn't open his eyes. The mental freak turned his head so that his good eye could see who'd entered. Charles moved with a penguin's grace as he crossed the room to stand in front of the chained man.

Windsor hung against his chains, his arms above his head and his feet against the chain link fence behind him. He was leaning forward, putting pressure on his joints, but taking them off his feet. Charles wouldn't let him lie down. He'd had to choose over the past four days what hurt. His joints, or his feet and legs.

"You said Titan was coming to kill me," Charles said. "Where the fuck is he?"

Windsor breathed heavily, like a fallen horse which had been ridden too hard for too long.

"Answer me," Charles said.

"I didn't say when," Windsor whispered, each word harder to say than the last.

Charles raised his hand, prepared to slap the hell out of the man. He didn't bring it down because something occurred to him. "*You.*"

Windsor swung slightly against his chains.

"You're going to talk to him. That's what I'm missing here. You'll tell him to come and he'll listen. This has all been about you anyway, hasn't it? This whole *fucking* war was for you, in some psychotic way. So, you'll talk, and he'll listen." Charles dropped his hand. "You understand?"

Windsor smiled, his swollen lips sliding bloodily across his teeth. "I'll talk to him, but Luke listens to no one."

ON PURPOSE AND OTHER THINGS

Thanks for reading, and I mean that wholeheartedly. I love telling stories and without you, that wouldn't be possible.

I know at the end of books, a lot of writers offer you something free if you sign-up for their mailing list. What they're doing, essentially, is buying your email address.

I don't want to do that.

I think having a purpose in life is important. It adds clarity and meaning to what you do. I'm lucky to know mine and that purpose dictates my life: I'm here to tell stories. Nothing else even comes close to the happiness this job gives me.

With that said, if you like reading my novels and want to know when the next book comes out, sign-up below. No tricks. No buying your address. Just me telling stories and you enjoying them.

The way these relationships should work.

Join Here:
https://www.subscribepage.com/danielscott

CONNECT WITH THE AUTHOR

Join Daniel's Email List here:

https://www.subscribepage.com/danielscott